D1583128

EMOTIONS

EMOTIONS

Claire Lorrimer

CHIVERS

British Library Cataloguing in Publication Data available

This Large Print edition published by BBC Audiobooks Ltd, Bath, 2009.
Published by arrangement with the author.

U.K. Hardcover ISBN 978 1 408 42119 2
U.K. Softcover   ISBN 978 1 408 42120 8

Printed and bound in Great Britain by
CPI Antony Rowe, Chippenham, Wiltshire

CONTENTS

1.

The Thirteenth Floor
Suspicion

Beneath my towelling beach robe my body was greasy with oil and I was looking forward to the fresh water shower I intended to take in my room after two sweltering hours on the sun terrace by my Madeira hotel swimming pool.

The lobby of the hotel was cool, dark, and nearly empty as I waited for the lift that was on its way down to collect me. It, too, was cool and dimly lit in contrast to the brilliance of the September sun. Thankfully I pressed the button and sped silently towards my floor.

As happened quite often, I had forgotten to take my room key down to the pool and I had to make my usual search along the corridor to find one of the Portuguese chambermaids who would oblige, as always, by letting me into my corner bedroom with a master key.

I muttered my customary *'obrigado'*—the only Portuguese word I knew, as the door was opened for me. Drunk with sunshine and late afternoon torpor, I walked into my room.

My heart missed a beat. The fitted wardrobe that opened on to the right of the tiny hallway leading to my bedroom was full of clothes—not my own few pairs of slacks and

1

solitary lounge suit, but soft, colourful feminine dresses, T-shirts, and a diaphanous white blouse. So my wife had arrived after all!

We had originally planned this two-week holiday as a last attempt to make a go of our five-year marriage—a kind of reconciliation honeymoon. At the eleventh hour, Barbara's daughter by her first marriage had developed one of her imaginary 'attacks' which, as my plump twelve-year-old thoroughly spoilt stepdaughter knew very well, would prevent her devoted mama from leaving her.

'I'll join you in a day or two, Grant!' Barbara had said, looking vaguely embarrassed but utterly determined. Seeing my expression, she added, 'I promise.'

I don't know whether I really wanted her to come with me or not. In more honest moments of self-searching, I was prepared to admit Barbara had married me on the rebound when her first husband Colin left her. If she really knew the meaning of the word love, physical or mental, she certainly had never proved it to me. But stubbornly I, who had loved her so much, hated the idea of defeat; of having to write off the five years of our marriage as pointless, wasted weeks and months of life, of effort, of trying, of the love given. And they were wasted.

Now, despite everything, I felt a moment of triumph. Barbara had joined me on this beautiful island and we might yet find a way to make our marriage work.

I was in our bedroom, my eyes searching for her. No Barbara, but a surprising scatter of her garments everywhere—nylon tights and pink briefs on the floor, white sandals lying at angles where they'd been kicked off at random—the dressing table a clutter of make-up, powder, perfume, bottles. Total disorder— and Barbara the tidiest, neatest, most careful woman I'd ever known!

I was intrigued. Had my wife suddenly changed—discovered she loved me, wanted me, missed me and rushed out to be with me?

I stopped my search of the room as I heard water running into the bath. Now I knew where she was—bathing after the journey, hurriedly changing her clothes to be ready to meet me, looking her usual cool impeccable self, but inside, eager, anticipating, too excited to fold her underwear, place her shoes side by side. And her dresses were new, too. I didn't recognise any of them.

My heart was now beating furiously. The cautious cynicism which had shadowed everything connected with Barbara these last few years was swept away by a youthful excitement I'd not known since the days before our marriage—before I knew she could be so cold, so destructive. She had always looked incredibly exotic, sensuous, inviting. It had taken me years to admit that this was a complete anomaly and that I'd married a sexless, insensitive prude. Now, when I'd been on the point of giving up, Barbara, it seemed, was about to prove me wrong.

Quickly, I opened the bathroom door. Her back was towards me, only her dark hair and shoulders visible above the white foam of the scented bubble bath in which she was indulging. The noise of the water cascading from both taps must have drowned the noise I'd made opening the door because she did not turn but lifted one long tapering white arm to sponge water over her shoulder. It was, to me anyway, an unconsciously sexual movement as her breast rose above the foam.

I stepped forward and bent my head to kiss the back of her neck.

That was when the shot rang out which killed her.

*　　*　　*

Two hours later, I was still at the local police station in Funchal, still trying to make myself understood, still trying to understand. This much I did know. The woman in the bath was dead. It was not Barbara. The man who had shot her was her husband who had his own key to their room. He told the police he'd thought I was her lover.

You'll probably be wondering, as I did, what this strange woman—and her husband—was doing in my room. For a long while I tried to keep my sanity whilst I listened to the police, and my English interpreter, trying to convince me that it was not my room at all. Eventually they took me back to the hotel and proved it to me, and I realised what had happened—I'd pressed the wrong button in the lift and got out on the 13th instead of the 12th floor. As the layout of the rooms was identical on each floor, I'd automatically gone to the corner room believing it to be mine.

But it couldn't end there. Since it was not my room, the police said, and the door was locked, how had I got in? The lady was in the bath but must earlier have opened the door to me—or, as her husband had supposed, she'd given me a key.

Over and over again, I insisted they question the chambermaid who'd let me in. Unfortunately, she'd gone off duty and as she lived up the mountain in a poor home without a telephone, could not be questioned until next day.

By then, Barbara really did arrive. She was quite wonderful, telling the police I was an upright, utterly reliable husband who would not dream of having a mistress; finding an English lawyer who'd retired to live in Madeira and knew Portuguese and, more important, the law. By evening, my passport had been returned to me, my good name restored and I was free. Neat, tidy, unflustered, self-possessed and utterly efficient, my wife coped with every contingency. I don't think it crossed her mind I might really have been involved. She believed me without question.

So did we become reconciled? No! You see, although I know she believed me innocent, the whole crazy incident gave her the opportunity she'd been looking for to end our marriage. It was typical of me to have been so careless, she said, before she took the next flight home, to be so carried away by stupid romantic notions. Any right-minded husband would have known at once she never left her clothes in such abandoned disorder, let alone take a bath in the middle of the afternoon. She had given up now the hope that I'd grow up and out of my irrational sentimental ideas.

I don't think of her often—but when I do remember her, I like to think of that other room on the 13th floor with its feminine disorder, its perfume and the white shoulder in the foam bath, and how happy we might have been.

2.

Delia
Perception

It was the first Wednesday of the month. Mrs Paley had been studying the calendar and now she said:

'It's Diana's afternoon!'

I think she was trying to hide even from me the fact that she wasn't much looking forward to her eldest daughter's duty visit. Diana came on the first Wednesday of every month, no matter what the weather and despite any domestic crisis at home. Nobody would ever be able to accuse Diana of neglecting her mother, of being unreliable or undutiful. This was one of the reasons why Mrs Paley really didn't enjoy the occasion—and it *was* An Occasion since she seldom saw anyone from one day's end to the next. Except for me, of course. She knew it wasn't really love which brought Diana out on a gusty rainy day to spend an hour or so with her old mother.

'But then Diana never was very affectionate, even as a little girl,' Mrs Paley said aloud, her thoughts running parallel with mine. 'Oh, well, Delia, I suppose I'd better tidy up the room a bit.'

But she remained seated in her favourite chair by the fire, an old crocheted shawl across her knees. I was curled up on the window seat staring through the blurred wet glass across the chimney tops of the houses on the opposite side of the street. It was grey, damp and depressing outside, but the room was comparatively warm and cosy. It was made to seem even smaller than it was by the endless pieces of bric-á-brac and innumerable photos and mementos dear to old people.

'Dear Delia!' said Mrs Paley suddenly, smiling at me. 'Where would I be without you?'

Or I without you! I thought.

We might have begun one of our luxurious reminiscences of the old days but for the arrival of Diana. The years had filled out her figure to a plump matronliness. Her hair was already grey though she could not yet be fifty. Her face, wet from the rain, was red and shiny.

'Well, Mother, how are you?'

The brisk dictatorial voice seemed to fill the little room, destroying the peace and quiet. Mrs Paley looked suddenly even older and frailer as she smiled and allowed Diana to kiss her cheek.

Diana seated herself opposite her mother and spread out her hands to the indifferent warmth of the gas fire.

'It's very chilly in this room, Mother. I really

8

do think it most unwise of you to go on living here with your rheumatism and all those stairs. You can't go on living here alone.'

'But I'm not alone. I have Delia!'

Although Diana's back was turned to me, I knew there was a frown of deepest disapproval on her face. For a moment, I came near to hating her. But I'd never do that. If it weren't for Diana, all those years ago, I wouldn't be here now. I knew that. I might not like her but I would be grateful to her as long as I existed.

'Don't you see, Mother, it isn't good for you to be living like this? And if you won't consider your own welfare, what about mine? I'd be far less worried about you if you were under my roof—and it would save me these ghastly treks up to town every month.'

'You don't have to come, Diana. I'd quite understand.'

The argument pursued its usual course. The same conversation took up most of Diana's visiting times. It also ended as usual with Diana's voice raised partly in anger at being thwarted and partly in self-pity:

'Everyone thinks it's so odd, Mother. I'm always being asked why you don't live with us now the children are grown up. It looks as if I'm not prepared to offer you a home. It's so unfair.'

Perhaps if Diana really loved her mother, Mrs Paley might go to live with her. But she knew as well as I did that Diana was only acting from a sense of duty and because she minded so much about the opinion of her friends and neighbours. Diana always had been covetous of people's good opinions.

'She can't help it,' Mrs Paley said when Diana had at last left us in peace again. 'It's because she was so plain as a child. She wanted to be admired and she never was. That made her bossy—and aggressive, too. I suppose it was pretty frustrating for her, especially as Lydia was such a pretty little thing. Do you remember Lydia's hair, Delia? Pure gold.'

Diana's younger sister, Lydia, was married now with a teenage son and a daughter of seven. The last time Lydia had brought the children to visit their grandmother, Lydia's little girl, Ann, had been asking about me.

'I want Delia to come and play with me!' she said. 'She used to play with Mummy. Mummy told me.'

It was quite true that a very large part of my time in those days was devoted to playing games with Lydia. Lydia was a thin frail little girl, as often ill as not, and because she was so frequently in bed, I was the one who helped to while away the time.

Between Diana and Lydia there was Eric. He had emigrated to Canada, and after Lydia, came little Ian, the fourth child. He, too, had emigrated—to Australia.

He was always a sensitive, very affectionate

little boy and I spent almost as much time with him as I had with Lydia, especially at night. A nervous, highly imaginative child who hated the dark, he usually wanted me to sit with him until he fell asleep. He used to believe that I warded off nightmares.

There was another child, too, in those days—baby Ann. She was barely a year old when she contracted meningitis and died. Lydia's little girl was named after her.

I don't think Diana or Eric had much time for me even when they were little, and they behaved as if I didn't exist at all. But when Diana needed me, she was willing enough to acknowledge me.

'No, I won't play Ludo!' she'd say irritably to Lydia. 'Let Delia play. She can have the blue counters and you have the red.'

I suppose Eric used me, too. But in a more humorous way than Diana. If there were a lost shoe or spilt paint-water, he would say it was my fault. I didn't mind being blamed. I rather liked Eric. In fact, I was miserable the first holidays after he'd been away to boarding school and came back very manly and grown up and wouldn't have anything to do with me.

'You know, Delia,' Mrs Paley said now, 'I think I'll have a look through the old photograph album. No matter what Diana says, I'm absolutely sure that child in the centre of the group by the croquet lawn is you.'

I suppose of all the things Mrs Paley and I

11

think and talk about, looking at the old snapshot album is one of our favourite pastimes. I knew perfectly well which photo she was referring to. It fascinated me because if what she said was true, it was the only time I could ever see myself.

We studied the photo carefully. Diana was on the extreme right, freckled, pig-tailed and unsmiling. Eric was beside her, Lydia and Ian kneeling on the grass in front of them with the baby, Ann, just a bundle in a carrycot by their legs. Between Diana's and Eric's faces, there is another girl, not quite in focus. As the photo is not in colour, one cannot see if the girl's hair is red, like mine.

Diana swears it isn't a face at all but a trick of the camera. She says the way her own head and Eric's are positioned, the space between could be just a gap in the foliage of the tree behind them.

But Lydia, when Mrs Paley pointed it out to her, laughed delightedly and said:

'But of course that's Delia.'

'Diana's always furious when I say it is you!' Mrs Paley said to me now, just a little spitefully.

I know it's difficult not to feel that way about Diana but it's a little different for me than for Mrs Paley. I do owe my life to Diana.

'Strange, isn't it, the way you became part of the family,' Mrs Paley said as she stared down at the picture. 'The children were all

12

convalescing after the measles. It was raining, just the way it is today. They were so bored—Diana most of all. She was scribbling in an exercise book when she suddenly said: "Do you realise that the first letter of each of our names makes another name—Delia—Diana, Eric, Lydia, Ian, Ann, D.E.L.I.A.!" "It's a nice name" Lydia said. "I wish I had a friend called Delia; someone who'd play with me. *Why* won't you play with me, Diana?"'

This was an old story oft repeated but I never tired of hearing it. Mrs Paley sighed and continued:

'"Delia can play with you instead," Diana said. She was always very good at getting out of doing something she disliked. "Delia has red hair, so she can have the red counters to match her hair." "And I'll have the yellow ones to match mine!" said Lydia.' Mrs Paley paused and looked up from the photo album and smiled at me.

'In no time at all, Lydia had you sitting on the end of the bed in a pretty blue velvet frock playing Ludo with her.'

I remembered. Lydia was so pleased because she won.

Mrs Paley smiled. 'That was one of the nice things about you, Delia. You always let the little ones win their games. Of course, that wasn't the only reason they loved you. Ian would only settle at night if you were going to sit with him until he fell asleep. You became so much part of the children's lives—and mine, too.' Mrs Paley mimicked Lydia's voice:

'"I want *two* toffees, Mother—one for Delia!" And then Eric's: "Delia knocked the croquet ball into the goldfish pond, Mother. I didn't!" Sometimes I could see you running across the lawn with the others, in your blue dress, your red hair flying in the wind. And do you remember when Diana told me she had pushed you into the lake and I was out onto the terrace in a panic before I realised it was a fib.'

'Diana could be hurtful sometimes!' I broke in. 'But I don't think she meant it. She just wanted to draw attention to herself.'

'Yes, she was jealous of Eric and Lydia and the little ones. Even now, when she's nearly fifty, she's still a little jealous because she knows I'm perfectly happy here in this room with you. She tries to convince me that I'm becoming senile. "Delia's simply a figment of your imagination, Mother," she says. "Why won't you admit it?"'

Mrs Paley sighed.

'Diana didn't understand how lonely I was after my dear husband died and the children left home. We'd lost all our money in the slump and it wasn't easy for me at first living alone here on my old-age pension. Then— then I remembered you and . . . you were so good, dear. You came at once.'

She smiled at me as she added:

14

'I do need you, Delia, just the way the children needed you when they were young. You're such a comfort to me, my dear. So kind! So pretty!'

I went and stood in front of the mirror but there was no one there.

3.

First Love
Fortitude

*For Tony, who shall be nameless but
who may recognise and remember himself.*

It was a very hot day. The August sun beat
down suffocatingly on the tiled roof of the
garage loft, making the interior like an oven.
We looked at one another and, by unspoken
agreement, stubbed out our dried grass, home-
rolled cigarettes and descended to the
comparative cool of the garage below.

Once again, the cold stiff corpse of Tony's
pet white rat met our uneasy gaze. I was glad
that Jeremy, rolled in a ball in my shorts'
pocket, was warm and vibrant, unlike the
stiffened Penelope. Our conference, held, like
all such of importance, had so far proved
sterile. We could not make up our minds
whether to bury Penelope or whether to skin
and stuff her, so preserving at least her
likeness for always.

We were both in favour of taxidermy. The
difficulty lay in who should perform this tricky
operation. Tony had sharpened his penknife to
a razor's edge but neither of us could stomach

the role of surgeon.

We had both been devoted to Penelope; Tony, of course, even more so than me since she was his pet. He'd greeted my arrival soon after breakfast with suspiciously red eyes which, tactfully, I had ignored. In an effort to cheer him up and make Penelope's death seem a little less final, I had suggested the stuffing operation.

I loved Tony with all the passion of a brotherless ten-year-old; I had always believed, until this moment, that I would do anything in the world for him. But sticking a penknife into that small white corpse was more than I could bring myself to do. I was deeply ashamed, as disappointed in myself as I thought Tony must be with me.

'We could make a beautiful coffin this morning and have a real burial service this afternoon!' I suggested tentatively. Tony had started carpentry lessons at his prep school last term and had proudly shown me a box he'd made.

He pushed his fair hair, damp from the heat, away from his forehead and stopped frowning at me.

'I suppose we could,' he answered. I knew the merest shades of his voice and was not deceived by the casualness of his tone.

We were soon hard at work. We used Jeremy for sizing up the coffin and to our delight, he fitted perfectly. The box, though rickety, was nonetheless a box complete with lid to be hammered in at the last minute.

'We ought to paint it now!' Tony said, perspiring but happy.

But we had no paint. All that was available was a can of green paint in the potting shed. Tony had been forbidden to use it because, the gardener told him, it contained arsenic which was a deadly poison.

'It's a blasted shame!' said Tony, who only swore when he was deeply moved. 'The paint would have finished off the job properly and Penelope *deserves* something nice.'

I saw my chance to vindicate myself in his eyes.

'I haven't been forbidden to use it,' I said. Our eyes met and Tony grinned.

We finished the painting as the lunch gong sounded.

One minute I was surveying the attractive display of cold chicken and fruit salad with a mouth-watering appetite. The next, my stomach had curled into a knot and I knew I couldn't eat a thing. Fortunately Tony's mother was out and the cook, who had charge of us, did not think to supervise our meal. Tony ate enough for two.

I was feeling too sick to watch him. I stood by the window staring at the green grass, the green leaves, the green hedges and remembered the green paint. Arsenic. Deadly poison.

No! I thought. I don't want to die!

I pushed the idea away from me and followed Tony back to the garage. Somehow, I helped him place Penelope's body, now wrapped in one of his father's silk handkerchiefs, into the green coffin. Somehow I stood upright, my stomach knotted with pain, while he dug a hole. Somehow I read the burial service from a prayer book. Tony filled in the hole and looked up at me.

'What's the matter with you?' he asked. 'You're green.'

'I feel sick,' I said as my legs buckled beneath me and I collapsed on the grass beside the grave. 'And I have a terrible pain.'

Tony sat down beside me, regarding me anxiously.

'Perhaps it's the paint and you've been poisoned,' he suggested. And then, as the thought struck him, 'if the grown-ups find out, they'll cane me.'

A wave of pain engulfed me. When it lessened, I gasped:

'I won't tell, I promise.'

'Cut your throat and hope to die?'

It was our usual vow but an unfortunate one in this instance. I had no doubt now that I *was* going to die. The pain came in regular spasms increasing each time in intensity. Every ten minutes or so I vomited on the lawn. Tony informed me, but without much hope, that there was no sign of green paint.

19

Slowly, inexorably, the afternoon wore on. The sun moved over to the west leaving our patch of lawn in the shade. I was burning hot.

'Perhaps I ought to tell Cook,' Tony suggested every now and again. 'She could telephone for the doctor or something!'

But I wouldn't let him.

'I was the one who took the paint,' I reminded him. 'I'd be punished, too.' I'm sure it never occurred to him that what I was suffering then was worse than any punishment a grown-up could inflict.

At six o'clock my mother came to collect me. Somehow I managed to smile, to wave to Tony, to put on an act of cheerful good health. I don't remember the drive home. My next recollection was of the doctor saying to my mother:

'Acute appendicitis . . . into hospital at once . . . operate tonight!'

I knew his diagnosis was wrong. I wanted desperately to shout out that I was dying from arsenic poisoning and that taking my appendix out couldn't possibly save my life. But I'd promised . . . I'd die rather than have Tony caned.

'Now see if you can count up to twenty. Breathe deeply . . . there now, don't be frightened . . . one, two, three . . .'

I came round some time later. I was in a private room in the cottage hospital, the nurse told me. My appendix had safely been removed and I was going to be just fine. I drank some water and went back to sleep.

Next morning I saw my scar. It was small, neat and had two metal clamps holding the edges of the incision together. I no longer had any pain. I no longer felt sick. I lay waiting for my mother's promised visit, wondering if the arsenic had drained out of me alongside the appendix. Was arsenic green? Would the surgeon have noticed it?

I questioned my mother in a roundabout way. It appeared that there was nothing unusual about my operation except that my condition had flared up so suddenly.

'Could I see Tony?' I asked.

He came next day. I showed him the scar and he was duly impressed by the clamps. He told me I was stupid not to have asked them to keep my appendix in a bottle.

'We could have looked at it, silly, to see if it was green,' he said. He didn't look very pleased with me and I felt vaguely depressed as he wandered away and stared out of the window. I couldn't think of anything we could do which would amuse or entertain him.

'I suppose we were a bit silly to use that paint!' he said at last. 'But . . . did anyone ask about . . . did you . . . ?'

'No,' I said. 'I didn't tell.'

He turned round from the window and grinned.

'No!' He picked a bit of fluff off the red

blanket and screwed it between his finger and thumb into a tiny ball. 'I didn't think you would. I told the guys at school you were as good as any boy!'

There was nothing much more to be said. Tony was soon bored with the sickroom visit and left me to make the best of my convalescence.

I lay in my bed remembering: *'As good as any boy.'* It was the highest accolade he could award me. I hugged my sore stomach, more than content.

This story appeared in Claire's autobiography 'You Never Know' as part of her childhood memories.

4.

Branch Line
Determination

Amanda glanced at her watch. With an audible sigh of resignation, she realised that it would be another five minutes before the branch line train for East Grensham would shudder, groan and finally leave the junction. She had forgotten momentarily that the three grimy, old-fashioned carriages always waited here for the London train to disgorge its home-going passengers. For the moment, she had the small, closed compartment to herself; no one to distract her thoughts. In less than half an hour, she would be home and still she had not made up her mind what she would say to her parents.

'Mum, Dad—I've left Gareth.'

'Gareth and I made a mistake—we should never have got married.'

'Would it be all right if I came home for a while?—I'm going to divorce Gareth.'

No, nothing she said would stop the look on their faces, the questions, and she was too tired, too over-wrought to cope. Perhaps it would be best not to tell them right away. Unfortunately they thought the world of Gareth and it wouldn't be easy convincing them how . . . how utterly impossible he was;

23

how he argued; complained; fought over the silliest things. Their rows were always over such stupid things—and they'd got worse and worse until—

The carriage door opened and an elderly lady struggled in with two large shopping bags. She settled herself on the seat opposite Amanda and smiled.

'I thought I was going to miss the train,' she said as the engine groaned into life and they jolted forwards. 'How nice to find you here, my dear. I always try to find a seat where there is at least one other woman. Richard, my husband, is adamant about it—so many dreadful things happening on trains these days.'

She paused for breath and smiled once more—such a sweet beaming expression that, despite her inner turmoil, Amanda smiled back.

'I'm going to East Grensham—are you?' her companion enquired. When Amanda nodded, she continued: 'Do you know, even after all these years, Richard still says: "Don't forget, five stops!" That's because I once did forget and he thought I was lost, poor darling. He doesn't seem to realise I'm only in my seventies and quite able to manage without him.'

She paused to peer inside one of the carrier bags and withdrew a small jeweller's box. 'He wanted to come with me but I wanted his

24

present to be a surprise. It's our golden wedding anniversary tomorrow. Would you like to see what I chose?'

Not wishing to be unkind, Amanda feigned an interest in the gold cigar cutter. Her companion gave a little laugh that sounded surprisingly girlish.

'I know he'll like it—it has a rather special meaning, you see. When we first married, Richard used to smoke all over the house and I hated it. Well, we had terrible rows about it and then we found a compromise. He gave up cigarettes and smoked cigars instead because I've always liked the smell of cigar smoke. Are you married, my dear? Yes, of course, you're wearing a wedding ring! I do hope you'll have as wonderful a marriage as Richard and I have. I expect it sounds silly to you coming from an old lady like me, but we're even more in love now than we were fifty years ago. We were so very lucky to find each other.'

'Yes! Fifty years is a long time. But . . . ' Amanda enquired ' . . . if you don't mind me asking, you said just now that you used to have terrible rows with your husband, so . . . so they can't all have been happy years.'

The old lady leaned forward and patted Amanda's hand.

'But of course they weren't—marriage isn't like that. You think when you leave the church that it will all be so simple because you love each other; but learning to live together is never easy. We fought like cat and dog over nearly everything. We each wanted our own way, you see.'

'And did you never . . . well, think of leaving him?'

'Of course I did—many times; but our generation believed in the vows we made—for better AND for worse. We saw it as a lifetime commitment—and so we struggled to make a go of it and gradually we both learned to give as well as take. It's different today, I know, but Richard and I always say when we read the divorce statistics—what a pity! If they'd only tried a little harder—a little longer, they might have found their way to the kind of happiness we have. It's a question of tolerance, don't you think? And if two people love each other and have the will to find a way, real love is worth the effort, the sacrifices, and the bad times. But then, you've probably not experienced the need yet. Ah, we're stopping! You're not getting out, are you? I thought you were going all the way to East Grensham?'

'No, but it was so nice meeting you—talking to you. I hope you will have a lovely day tomorrow.'

Doors were opening, closing. Amanda stepped down on to the platform and made her way towards the ticket office. If she'd only known, she would have bought a return ticket. Now she would have to buy a single back to London.

She turned as the train chugged its way under the bridge and disappeared round the curve in the track.

'Goodbye—and thank you!' She muttered as she went to peer at the train departure board. With a little luck—and this must surely be her lucky day—she would be back in London by five thirty and Gareth need never know where she had been.

5.

The Good Samaritan
Revenge

It was quiet that morning in the dining room. Usually Jean, the young girl who was the dogsbody in Mrs Bestman's boarding house and waited at table, was clattering around with dishes, chattering in her cheerful way to each of the elderly residents she served. Mrs Bestman, having no time for and no trust in the younger generations, only took in retired people. Her lodgers had the advantages of being both permanent and on small private pensions for which they had become eligible on retirement. This meant she could be comfortably sure of regular payment.

In all, there were six residents—all deemed by Mrs Bestman to be highly respectable and unlikely to give her any trouble. Nor, in the two decades or so since she had been widowed and decided to take in boarders, had she had trouble of any kind. There had been one occasion when old Miss Dove, a one time governess to the children of a Belgian family, had been found by Jean unconscious in her bedroom and had been rushed off to hospital with pneumonia—a drama which had prompted Mrs Bestman to the unusual step of producing glasses of sherry for the remaining residents who had watched the arrival and departure of the ambulance from the lounge window.

There had been only one other disaster Mrs Bestman could recall when a dirty, pony-tailed youth, unshaven and in filthy clothes, had called to see Mr Menforth, the former chemist, claiming to be his illegitimate son and desperately in need of money to buy drugs. The youth was one of the psychiatric patients who had been released into the community to fend for himself and who had happened to sit next to Mr Menforth in the doctor's surgery and followed him back to Mrs Bestman's boarding house.

Poor Mr Menforth had been deeply embarrassed, no less so when Mrs Bestman had felt obliged to call the police to remove the aggressive mental patient from her doorstep and all the neighbours as well as the residents had observed with some excitement this brief 'Crimewatch' event.

With such a remarkably unadulterated reputation, it was all the more shocking therefore, when on Thursday, the 18th of December, one of Mrs Bestman's elderly lodgers murdered another. Perhaps that was putting it a little too strongly, Mrs Bestman conceded, when relating the event to her sister some time later. But there was little doubt, according to the Coroner's verdict, that Mr

Ainsley, the erstwhile toy salesman, would be alive now were it not for what was said that breakfast time on the day Jean failed to come to work.

It so happened that Jean, poor girl, was laid low with 'flu and Mrs Bestman had been obliged to serve breakfast herself. This would not have had any bearing on subsequent events except that normally, when Jean arrived for work in the mornings, she always brought with her the lodgers' newspapers—the *Daily Mail* for Miss Dove, the *Express* for Mr and Mrs Ivanitch, the refugee couple, the *Guardian* for Mr Ainsley and two *Telegraphs*—one for Mr Menforth and one for Mr King, the former schoolmaster.

Both these gentlemen, Mrs Bestman explained to her sister, were avid crossword enthusiasts. It would be hard to tell which was the more obsessive. When Mr Menforth had first come to stay, Mr King had been delighted to find a fellow enthusiast. For years they competed every morning to see who could complete the crossword first. Sometimes it would be one, sometimes the other. At Christmas time, Mrs Bestman allowed a small bet on the outcome just to give the rivalry a little zest.

Jean, who was a kind-hearted girl, was aware, as were all the residents, of this friendly rivalry; and to be fair, she would take it in turns to which elderly man she gave his paper

30

first. 'Your turn today, Mr King!' she would say with her cheeky smile, or: 'Got your biro ready, Mr Menforth?' And at lunchtime, she would always enquire who'd been the winner that day; and if there was any pudding left over, that one would receive the extra helping.

It was all harmless fun, Mrs Bestman said. Of course, pride did creep into it sometimes. Mr King, being a schoolteacher, liked to think he had the edge over Mr Menforth, but old age was beginning to slow his mental processes and he worried lest the dreaded onslaught of Alzheimer's was causing him to lose his memory. Mr Menforth was ten years younger, which did give him a slight advantage, or so the late Mr Ainsley maintained. A loud-voiced, booming fellow, immensely good-natured, Mr Ainsley had, in his salesman's days, been nicknamed The Good Samaritan. It was he who had taken control when Miss Dove had been found unconscious; he who was always ready with an umbrella when someone had lost theirs; who would offer to go out on a rainy day to collect their pensions from the post office; who would take their books back to the library. In fact Mr Ainsley was the one Mrs Bestman turned to when the pipes froze or the gas cooker failed to function. He always knew what to do and was ready with a helping hand.

'That's why I simply can't understand the Coroner!' Mrs Bestman said to her sister. 'Of

31

all people, Mr Ainsley was the kindest, and he was really only trying to help. Needless to say, on that fatal day it was he who went to the newsagent to get the papers Jean hadn't been able to collect. Miss Dove was sitting next to Mr Menforth so she saw it all happen and in the end, it was her evidence the Coroner took most note of.

'It was like this,' she went on. 'Over the years both gentlemen had agreed to certain rules. They didn't start doing their crosswords until after breakfast although they could look at the clues during their meal. They couldn't use dictionaries and no information of any kind must be exchanged although they could comment about their progress. One might say: "Having a bit of bother with 14 Down?" Or "Have you solved 3 Across yet?" But that was as far as it went. They were both remarkably good at solving clues and it was a rare day they didn't complete the puzzle. If either one couldn't do so, the other was automatically the winner that day and gained a point. If neither completed, then they would compare notes and neither could add to their overall score. On the day of Mr Ainsley's death, Mr Menforth was two games behind in the overall total. "It was irking him a bit," Miss Dove maintained, "being so near Christmas when the grand total for the year was announced and everyone applauded the winner." Although that was just her opinion.

'But I do know for a fact he wasn't himself,' Mrs Bestman continued, 'because he'd not touched his sausage that morning and only picked at the beans and that was his favourite breakfast. I'd gone out to the kitchen to get some more coffee for the Ivanitches so I didn't see what happened, but Miss Dove told the Coroner that events went like this. When Mr Ainsley brought in their papers, both gentlemen opened theirs and looked at the clues. Mr Menforth went first white and then quite pink. "Reckon I'll get a game back today!" he'd told Miss Dove, beaming. "18 Across is a chemical clue—one I doubt very much indeed our friend will be able to answer!" It was at that point Mr Ainsley said in his loud voice: "Ran into the pharmacist in the newsagent. Nice fellow! Said to tell you chaps the answer to 18 Across is . . . " "Don't tell us. Don't tell us," Mr Menforth gasped, but obviously Mr Ainsley didn't hear him. "Eutectic!" he said. "Something to do with melting at low temperatures . . . " That's when Mr Menforth stood up, grabbed his knife and stuck it into Mr Ainsley's heart.'

Mrs Bestman paused to clear her throat. 'Mr Menforth must have just gone off his head,' she said. 'I call it a dreadful accident. Personally, I can't see how it had anything to do with the crosswords despite what the Coroner said, can you? After all, poor Mr Ainsley was only doing one of his usual kind deeds.'

6.

The Mistress
Heartache

She lay in the bath, studying her body, trying to imagine that it belonged to some other woman. Slim, supple, rounded, the pink nipples showing just above the water level; pink varnished toenails of one foot extended to touch the silver tap. Beautiful? Perhaps. Desirable? Yes, he would find her so. She held her breasts, cupping them in her hands as, soon, he would do. Her eyes closed and she permitted herself the luxury of anticipatory dreams.

When first he arrived he would be taut, nervous, overcome by the impatience of his desire. She thought of his male body, erect, demanding, possessive and her female body weakening in reply. How she would love him! All morning she had felt the love inflamed by desire, igniting within her and ready now to burst into a white-hot flame. Every part of her longed for him, wanted him, needed him, loved him. It seemed impossible that there was still an hour, sixty minutes to be endured before he would arrive and take her in his arms and at last, at last, she could love him as no woman had ever loved him before.

She found herself praying: 'Come soon! Come early! Surprise me, my love, and come to me now. Oh, how I will love you, kiss you, hold you, touch you.'

The waiting was almost unbearable.

She climbed out of the bath, dried herself slowly on a huge white towel and powdered her body from a distance, blowing it onto her skin where every nerve end was aching with the intensity of her longing.

The telephone rang.

'Tamara, how are you, my darling?'

'Darling, so full of love for you. Where are you? Are you coming soon?'

'Not quite as soon as I had hoped. You see, the Molinskis have asked me to take them water-skiing. It is such a perfect day and as you know, they have no boat, so I could hardly refuse. You understand, my dearest one, don't you?'

'When will you be here?'

'Perhaps four, or soon after. I love you so much. Do you realise, love-of-my-life, that it's one whole week since I last held you in my arms?'

'Yes, yes, I know!'

'Do you love me?'

'Yes, yes, I do!'

She replaced the receiver and lay down on the bed. Presently the beating of her heart slowed and the tension in her body drained away leaving it empty and cold. Now there was nothing in her but the raging torment of her thoughts.

When finally he arrived, she was dressed, on the balcony. She stood up to greet him. He took her in his arms. His hair was wet and salty from the sea. He wore only beach trunks and a blue towelling shirt. His lips were warm, demanding.

'How cool you are—and beautiful, as always. You cannot imagine, Tamara, how much I want you.'

He kissed her again, his hands pushing down the straps of the white dress, revealing her brown shoulders and the upward curve of her breasts. He bent his head and his kisses burned her skin.

'What's wrong? Don't you want to make love? How cold you are—pale, golden, but cold. Why are you always like this? I thought you wanted me. We've not made love for a whole week yet you stand there like Venus, carved in marble. Don't you want me?'

'Of course, of course!' she lied.

She lay beneath him, imprisoned in the icy cave of her mind. From far away, she watched his strong brown hands on her body; watched the gradual response of her physical self and the tears stung like salt water at the back of her eyes.

'Was it good for you, too, dearest? My love, my darling!'

'Yes!'

His lips on her cheeks tasted the tears she had not after all been able to withhold.

'What's wrong? Why are you crying? Wasn't it right for you? What is the matter? You're different. You've changed. Once you were so happy, always laughing, always fun. Why do you cry? Is there some other man? Is that why you were so cold to me when I arrived? Don't deny it, Tamara. I'm not insensitive, you know. I can feel that you've changed. Don't you love me any more? What have I done to upset you? Is it something I've said? Tell me!'

'It's nothing, nothing!' she said. 'There is no other man. It's you I love.'

She reached up her hands and cupping his face, kissed him tenderly on the lips.

He smiled, reassured.

'How strange you are!' He said presently. 'You are so many different Tamara's. I'm never sure how I will find you. What makes you behave sometimes in such a strange way?'

You, she thought. I am an instrument. Because I love you, I respond only to your touch. I am what you make me. One careless touch and I produce only discord. A loving touch and I am capable of being all that you desire. I can give you harmony, a great glowing melody, an opera, a concerto, a symphony of love. But you are like a child who hasn't yet learned to play with mature understanding. You are a child, playing with love and I am afraid. I am filled with a cold, terrible fear, because I have placed my woman's heart into your hands.

'I must go in a little while,' he said. His cheek rested on her shoulder.

'So soon?'

'I'm afraid I must,' he answered regretfully. 'It's so beautiful, so peaceful lying here. I wish I need never leave you. But I will return soon, my darling. A week apart is far, far too long. I will try to get away at the weekend when I shouldn't be so busy. Always there seem to be tiresome duties to keep me from you.'

Nothing, nothing would keep me from you, she thought.

'Why do you turn your face away from my kiss? There are times I really do not understand you, Tamara. It's true you can show more warmth, more passion than any woman I've ever known, but there are times when, if I didn't know you better, I would call you frigid.'

Dear God, she thought. Dear God! Please make him stop speaking.

'Your behaviour the other day at the Morinskis was extraordinary to say the least. There was no excuse for it, no reason whatever.'

Why can't he understand that I was frighteningly jealous; wretchedly insecure? If he had only shown one sign of love, one . . .

'You're not even listening to me, Tamara. Surely you realise how serious this is? It could ruin everything there is between us. How can you expect me ever to feel the same about you after such an ordeal?'

'You know how sorry I am.'

But it couldn't have been any different. Only he could have made it otherwise; a look, a word, a touch, invisible to others but enough to give her the reassurance to calm her rising hysteria. How hopeless it really was! He loved her because she was a passionate, emotional woman but the very sensitivity that made passion and emotion possible also created hysteria. Security was calming, but with this lover there was no security. Love was calming, but in front of the Morinskis he showed no love.

'We'll say no more about it. After all, it wasn't like you at all.' Surprisingly he laughed. 'In a way, it was my own fault. I had talked too much about you, telling them how vivacious, how charming, how fascinating you were. If I'd said nothing beforehand, I should not have felt such a fool when you presented yourself quite differently.'

'Perhaps it would be better if you didn't in future introduce me to your friends. I find it difficult to be natural; to behave as if there were nothing between us.'

He leant on one elbow and looked down at her, his eyes burning.

'But I want them to see you, know you. I'm so proud of you, darling. I wish I could present you to the whole world as mine. There are times when I feel I cannot endure life without you. You mean everything that is important to me. Without you, my life would seem quite pointless, meaningless. I know that I don't really deserve you. You are wasting your life with me. I ought to give you up but you are far, far too dear to me. I need you, Tamara. I need you.'

Now at last the ice around her heart was beginning to melt. The first sweet tones swept down the nerve-strings into her body in warm, gentle waves. Her hands tightened around his waist as the exigency of desire began its first torment of longing.

'You are my world, my real life. I love you, Tamara. I love you . . . '

Now the instrument was alive to the tiniest nuance of the player. Now, at last, mind and body were merged in a tempestuous surge of abandon. She was free at last to give; ready now to take.

'I love you! I want you . . . '

'I want you, too, darling, but I shall have to go. Time spent with you goes so quickly. Why, I'm half an hour late already. Mix me a drink, Tamara, while I take a shower. God, how hot it was on the beach this afternoon but the water was superb. Perhaps we can go swimming together later in the week if I can get away . . . '

She put on a bathrobe and mixed a Campari

and soda the way he liked it, with plenty of ice. When he came out from the bathroom, he paused to take the glass and kiss her. He was smiling.

Presently he dressed. He turned and put his arms round her.

'Wish I could stay longer,' he whispered against her hair. 'Perhaps, after all, there would be time . . .'

'No, no!' she said quickly. 'You'd only be sorry afterwards. You're late already.'

'You're so soft and warm and tempting. If we . . .'

'No,' she said again, and less sharply, 'no, darling, you'd better go.'

He sighed.

'Funny girl—a moment ago I could have sworn you . . . oh, well, maybe one of these days I'll understand women.'

He kissed her and she manufactured a smile.

'Happy?' he asked tenderly.

'Yes!' she lied.

7.

Mother Love
Guile

'Don't turn the light out . . . please, Mum, *please . . .*'

Clare's hopes of getting her young son to settle down for the night were dashed. It was already long past Fergus' bedtime and Andy would be home any moment wanting his supper. Fergus' fear of being left alone was a fairly new development and so far, warm drinks, a relaxing bath, and extra long bedtime stories had failed to be effective.

'Please, Mum, please . . . '

With a sigh, she walked back to the bed and sat down, her heart melting at the wistful expression in Fergus' huge blue eyes.

'Darling, I promise you there really isn't a single thing to be frightened about . . . '

'But what about the bears?' he interrupted. 'They might come and eat me.'

She drew a small sigh.

'There aren't any bears in this country,' she told him gently. 'Bears live in places like Canada and . . . '

'But there's bears in the zoo. We see'd them. Big brown ones—and a white cola bear.'

'Polar bear,' she corrected automatically. 'But Fergus, those bears in the zoo are in cages. They can't get out. They are safely locked in.'

'Yes, but s'posing it came undone—the gate, I mean, and a bear got out.'

Clare smiled reassuringly.

'Even if it did—and I've never heard of it happening, Fergus—the zoo is miles and miles away from our house.'

'But it could have walked and walked ever since last Christmas and it would be just about here by now.'

Clare glanced at her watch. It was nearly eight o'clock. She turned back to her son.

'Fergus, it's getting very late and Dad will be home any minute and want his supper. I must go and start cooking, but I'll leave the light on.' With a flash of inspiration, she added: 'Bears don't like lights so even if there was a bear in the garden, it wouldn't come in here.'

'But it might eat Bumper,' Fergus said anxiously, referring to his pet rabbit safely ensconced in a hutch by the garden shed.

Clare's voice rose a tone or two.

'Bears don't eat rabbits. They eat . . . ' she paused. What did bears eat? 'Honey,' she said. 'They like honey. Remember Winnie the Pooh? He liked honey.'

Fergus' expression was thoughtful. As she rose from the bed, he said: 'We've got honey in the kitchen. The bear might come in and eat it and still be hungry and . . . '

'And he'd be very grateful I'd let him have the honey and he'd say "thank you" and go away.'

'But bears can't talk.'

'This one can.'

'Did he go to school or did his Mum and Dad teach him?'

'Teach who what?' Andy's voice from the doorway startled both of them. 'And why aren't you asleep, young Fergus?'

Fergus sat up in bed and looked happily at his father.

'Because Mum's telling me a story about a bear what eats honey and can talk and . . . '

Andy looked sternly at his wife's guilty face.

'That's the third night in a row. Haven't you yet grasped what this rascal is up to? He's no more frightened of the dark than you or I are, are you, Fergus?'

Fergus snuggled down beneath the bedclothes, a grin on his face.

'No, but it's my fav'rite game. Last night I sawed a big green snake under the bed and . . . '

'. . . and that's the last time you'll trick Mum into believing you,' his father said, turning to look at Clare.

'But Andy, if he *is* frightened . . . '

'But he's not, are you, Monster?'

Fergus snuggled further down into his pillow, his eyes sleepy now as his father bent to kiss him goodnight.

'No, but it's a really good game,' he murmured. 'And my bear does like honey.

8.

The Summer of 1933
Compassion

Squidge and I were sitting in her garden listening to her two grandchildren discussing the appropriate age to start having sex. Squidge, my elder sister by one year and whose real name was Penelope, caught my eye. I knew exactly what she was thinking—Arthur her grandson was thirteen, Penny, her granddaughter, twelve—the same ages Squidge and I had been that summer of 1933.

'What age were you when you started, Gran?' Penny asked with total candour.

Squidge smiled.

'Children didn't have sex in our day—children stayed children. That isn't to say we didn't fall in love.'

She caught my eye again and Arthur, who'd noticed it, said quickly:

'Come on, Great Aunt—you must have known what Gran got up to. She said you did everything together until you left school.'

I looked questioningly at Squidge who nodded.

'Then I'll tell you about the summer of 1933 when we were your ages!' I said. 'But you won't believe it. The holidays had just started and our mother was going to take us to the seaside for two weeks. Then your great grandfather was rushed into hospital and our mother told us the holiday would have to be cancelled.

'I'm afraid you will have to spend the summer holidays with your Aunt Ivy!' Mother said. This announcement couldn't have been more of a bombshell—an unwelcome bombshell, and Squidge and I looked at each other in horror.

Squidge pleaded with Mother.

'But you know Aunt Ivy is one of our A.D's!' she gasped.

A.D. was part of our not-so-secret code. It stood for Actively Dislike. Then there was Q.L. for Quite Like and N.T.B. for Not Too Bad, and so on. We used it for assessing grown-ups who came to visit our parents when we were obliged to change into pretty dresses, tie our plaits in ribbons and use a scrubbing brush on our fingernails. Not only this but we had to sit quietly while the grown ups talked about U.B.—Utterly Boring—subjects until finally, after handing round teacups and plates of sandwiches, we were excused.

Neither of us noticed that Mother was looking pale and distressed as we gazed at her accusingly. We had sympathy only for ourselves, and, as Squidge said later when we repaired to our den in the loft over the shrubbery:

'It's not as if she didn't KNOW we can't

47

stick Aunt Ivy.'

Aunt Ivy was Father's elder brother, Bob's, second wife who, mercifully, we normally only saw at Christmas when all the family relations forgathered at their house, Uncle Bob being too incapacitated by his wartime disabilities to travel. He'd been badly gassed in the war and wheezed all the time but he was usually cheerful and always gave us a guinea to buy whatever we wanted so we'd given him a G.S. rating for being a Good Sport. But Aunt Ivy . . .

'Mother said it might not be for the WHOLE hols!' Squidge tried to console herself as well as me. 'Eight weeks—think of it, Titch!'

'Maybe poor Father isn't as bad as Mother thinks . . .'

Squidge and I were both devoted to our father and we'd been shocked by Mother's unguarded admission that he might never come out of hospital. Death was something we had not yet encountered—other than for our guinea pigs and Father's old Labrador—but the finality of it was something we preferred not to think about.

My sister, Squidge—your grandmother— was tall, leggy, blonde and pretty. She still is! I was short, thin with straggly straight brown hair and wore glasses for my short-sightedness. Squidge, who was not only my sister but my best friend, joined in my prayer every night for

God to make me grow tall and see properly without my tiresome spectacles, and Someone-up-There must have been listening, because although now I've remained petite in build, there was the miracle of contact lenses, so no one knew I was born blind as a bat, when I was of an age for it to matter.

One of the reasons I hated Aunt Ivy was because she never failed to draw attention to my 'deportment' as she called it, by which she meant my habit of hunching up my shoulders as I peered at a book or a plate of food.

'She only does it because she can't SEE properly!' Squidge used to defend me. 'It's not her FAULT!'

Squidge disliked her for other reasons. When Uncle Bob remarked how pretty she was growing and what a heart-breaker she would be one day, which was only the truth, Aunt Ivy would say: 'Don't put such silly ideas into the child's head, Robert. She's conceited enough already,'—which was not the truth. Squidge wasn't interested in her looks in those days and as we were both at an age to dislike boys, we'd made up our minds we would never get married, have husbands and children to bother us. Funny, really, when you think we've both defied these prophecies and been wonderfully happily married.

But I'm forgetting my story about the summer of 1933. We were packed off and sent down to Dorset in the care of a Universal

49

Aunt, to Great Oakmead, Uncle Bob's family home. It was a beautiful house—six times the size of our modest London abode, and although only Uncle Bob and Aunt Ivy lived in it, there was a retinue of servants—a butler, parlourmaid, housemaid, Uncle Bob's valet who'd been his batman in the war and Aunt Ivy's personal maid, Inez. Then there was Cook and a kitchen maid and Albert who saw to fires and cleaned shoes, and, of course, Matthews, the chauffeur who drove the Daimler when Aunt Ivy wanted to go shopping or visiting.

Squidge and I were given a suite of rooms on the third floor—once the nursery quarters when Uncle Bob had been a boy. We liked being up there with the schoolroom to play in on wet days and which was seldom visited by Inez, who never failed to complain about the mess or the noise we made, and sneaked to the grown ups about the tadpoles and dormouse we'd hidden in our bedroom. We thought her as old and crabby as Aunt Ivy herself, although looking back, I suppose neither was yet forty! Now Squidge and I are old (though I trust not crabby) we laugh at our child's eye view of age in those days.

For all we disliked Aunt Ivy, one thing quickly became clear to us as we settled in at Great Oakmead—Uncle Bob adored her. Squidge and I were hard put not to dissolve into fits of giggles when he called her by one of his many pet names—'Dearest One', 'My Little Sweetheart', 'My Angel'. Ugh! and he'd watch her move round the room with adoring, spaniel's eyes. 'It really is sickening!' Squidge said. 'If that's love, I certainly don't want it when I grow up!'

'It's not even as if she looked like an angel or a sweetheart,' I agreed. Aunt Ivy had crimped, Marcel-waved hair which she had bleached a brassy yellow with something we'd seen in her bathroom called Peroxide. She had a round face and big blue eyes fringed with spiky lashes, which she curled with a tiny pair of tongs before gluing them with black mascara. She was tall, long-waisted but with a big bosom which stuck out and both Squidge and I had sworn an oath that when we grew bosoms (we didn't talk of anything so factual as 'breasts' in those days) we'd squash them flat with bandages. Aunt Ivy actually seemed to like hers and on hot summer days, she would wear blouses or dresses with scooped out necklines and Uncle Bob used to stare at them with a silly smile on his face.

'I suppose he hasn't got much else to stare at,' Squidge said charitably. We both felt sorry for him, stuck in a chair all day with nothing but the wireless to listen to.

'You must try to entertain him, girls!' Mother had instructed us before the holiday started. 'It's not much of a life for the poor man—and he had a pretty rotten time in the war. Don't you young girls ever forget, he nearly lost his life helping to win the war. Thank God there'll never be another one!'

Of course, Mother didn't know then that the Second World War was only six years away and that Uncle Bob wouldn't live to see the end of it.

Uncle Bob liked to tell us stories about the war. He'd tell us the really gruesome parts about shooting rats and eating them; and finding soldiers' legs and arms and skulls when they'd had to dig new trenches. I don't think Squidge and I believed the half of it and Aunt Ivy was furious if she came in and heard him in the middle of one of his gory tales. She'd shake her finger and shout at him as if he was a child like us, and her scarlet painted mouth would open and shut until tears welled up in poor Uncle Bob's eyes. He never answered her back the way Squidge did once when Aunt Ivy threw her dormouse out of the window to its certain death.

'You're cruel and beastly and horrible!' Squidge said, too angry to cry although tears were misting up my glasses. 'I hate you and if Father wasn't so ill, I'd go home.'

It was one of those hot, August afternoons when Aunt Ivy decided the only possible punishment befitting the offence was to lock us in the nursery for the rest of the day.

'Whilst SHE goes out for a nice, cool drive!' Squidge said furiously as from the barred windows, we watched Aunt Ivy climb into the Daimler which had its roof folded down, and Matthews in his grey uniform and peaked cap drove off in regal style.

We both quite liked Matthews. The Daimler was garaged in one of the disused stables and as often as not, he'd bring it out into the cobbled yard and wash and polish it. Sometimes he'd let us help, although we weren't allowed to hold the hosepipe in case we soaked our dresses and Aunt Ivy saw what we'd been up to. She was always telling us 'not to be familiar with the servants'. We understood that by 'familiar' she really meant friendly, but it was impossible not to be friendly with Matthews.

He was quite young for a grown-up—only twenty-five—and we felt he was on our side rather than Aunt Ivy's. 'Dursn't let Her Ladyship find out you've been doing my work for me!' he'd say, although Aunt Ivy hadn't a title. 'Cost me my job you will!' He had laughing brown eyes and if it was really hot, he'd take off his shirt, and his chest and arms were as brown as a gypsy's—and as strong. He could whistle like a bird, and sing, in a deep baritone—ballads, mostly, though where he'd learned them we never knew.

Yes, Matthews was attractive in a very positive, male way and it wasn't long before Squidge decided that she might be 'in love' with him. We discussed it for hours because neither of us was really sure what being 'in love' meant. Squidge said she felt funny when he'd lifted her onto the bonnet and told her she was the prettiest mascot he'd ever seen. And she'd blushed. 'Had I felt anything like that when he'd handed me the polishing cloth and his hand had touched mine?' Squidge asked me. I could see she was disappointed when I said 'no'; but I promised to watch out for any funny signs next time we were in Matthews' company.

Perhaps it was the hot weather; or perhaps we were just beginning to grow up, but as the weeks went by, instead of talking about our chances of getting into the netball team or whether we'd be made prefects or pass our exams, Squidge and I spent a lot of time in the orchard of Great Meadows lying in the long grass, smelling the ripening apples, chewing grass stalks and talking about love and that forbidden topic, sex. We knew about The Curse because Sally, the nursery maid, had asked us if either one needed sanitary towels and after a lot of giggling, explained what they were and why girls of our age might need them. It was just as well because that summer, poor Squidge got what we called The Curse and she knew where to go for help. I was terribly upset, not because I wanted anything so unpleasant to happen to me, but because it somehow put an invisible barrier between Squidge and me, and there'd never been one

54

before.

Soon after this event, Squidge shocked me by announcing that she had changed her mind about never getting married—when she was grown up, she was going to marry Matthews.

'But you can't!' I cried. 'You just can't!'

'Why not?' Squidge argued, although I could see by her face that she wasn't as sure of herself as she was pretending.

'He's only a chauffeur!' I protested. 'If we marry anybody, it's got to be a doctor or a solicitor or a bank manager—someone like Father. You wouldn't be allowed to marry a CHAUFFEUR!'

Squidge looked as if she was going to cry.

'I don't see why not—not if we love each other,' she said.

'I don't think that's got much to do with it. Anyway, how do you know Matthews is in love with you?'

'It's the way he looks at me!' Squidge explained. 'It's in his eyes.'

I tried to see something distinctive in Matthews' eyes next time I saw him, but as I told Squidge, on scout's honour, I couldn't. We went round to the stable yard for me to have another look—but that's when it happened. Aunt Ivy came storming out of the house door into the yard and barred our way. There was no question about it—she was beside herself with anger. Her normally doll like pallor was purple and she shook her fist in Squidge's face and gabbled almost incoherently.

We made sense of some of it although we didn't realise the true explanation until after the holiday was over and Mother explained things to us. I don't suppose she would have done if something else hadn't happened—something that couldn't go without an explanation.

As usual when we'd transgressed, Squidge and I were confined to our rooms for disobeying—not once but on several occasions—Aunt Ivy's orders not to hobnob with the servants. Had we no idea how irritating it must be for Matthews to be pestered by two silly, tiresome, little girls? Did we not appreciate the position we put him in? How could he, our Uncle's employee, tell us to keep away from the stable yard and leave him in peace? What would our parents think? It was clear we were not to be trusted . . . and how many times had she told Squidge that she was to keep her hair in pigtails and not let it flow round her shoulders like some gypsy ragamuffin? It was high time we both learned some lady-like behaviour, and from now on, the stable yard was Out of Bounds.

Squidge dripped tears into the grubby handkerchief I gave her.

I tried to console her with a quotation from I knew not where but thought might be Shakespeare: *The path of true love never runs smooth*. It only made her sob louder. Then, as

I was about to give up hope, she suddenly stopped crying.

'I don't care WHAT she says. If I want to see Matthews, I will! I'll creep down when I know she's somewhere else. You can spy on her for me, Titch. Someone's got to tell Matthews it isn't my fault I can't see him any more. Maybe we can write to each other. I can give him our address at home and we can exchange letters until I'm old enough to marry him.'

It didn't seem the time to question whether Matthews was willing to wait that long—after all, Squidge was only thirteen and wouldn't be twenty-one for another eight years! And even if he did wait, it seemed unlikely Father would give them enough to live on and Squidge ought to know for herself that Father wouldn't approve of him. For one thing, he didn't use a handkerchief but wiped his nose on his sleeve; and he didn't speak the King's English but a kind of Dorset dialect. Worst of all, he used swear words like 'bloody'—well, only once when he got a puncture just when he was putting the car away, but even Squidge was shocked.

Squidge was urging me to go and see what Aunt Ivy was up to. I could use the servants' staircase—Aunt Ivy seldom did. If she did happen to see me I could say I was sneaking into the kitchen for a few biscuits or a piece of cake. Sally was always sympathetic when we were confined to the nursery without any tea or supper.

Wanting to help Squidge if I could, I undertook the task she had given me, though not without misgivings. Sally was in the kitchen and gave me both cake and biscuits, but she didn't know where Aunt Ivy was. I reported back to Squidge who'd recovered sufficiently to devour the food I'd bought.

'She's probably with Uncle Bob, telling him what horrible children we are,' I suggested.

'That's it then!' Squidge said, cramming the last piece of cake into her mouth. 'I'm going down to the yard now. You can stay here, Titch.'

'If you're going, I'm going,' I said staunchly. 'I can keep watch while you're talking to Matthews.'

Squidge hugged me and I knew I'd risk any sort of punishment to make her happy—well, happier, or so I thought.

We crept down the back staircase and out through the cloakroom into the garden. The lawn had been recently mown and the smell of sun-dried grass was so glorious and pungent, I can close my eyes now, after all these years, and still smell it. Squidge looked radiant with excitement and although I was still dubious about her mission, I have to say I was enjoying the escapade.

We edged round the vegetable garden wall and through the door into the yard. Only a dozen or so white doves disturbed the silence. The garage door was shut and, we discovered, locked. There was no sign of Matthews.

Squidge looked up at the clock tower and frowned.

'It's only five o'clock! He can't have gone off duty yet!' she said.

We decided to look in the tack room. Matthews sometimes went in there to smoke one of his Woodbine cigarettes. He'd even allowed us to have a puff once but neither of us liked it and we didn't ask for another. The tack room, too, was empty. That's when Squidge heard a noise—not a squeak or a moan but something between the two, she whispered. Holding my breath, I listened and heard it, too.

'Sounds like a kitten or something up in the hayloft,' I said. 'Perhaps it's trapped!'

We were both missing our guinea pigs and our dog which Aunt Ivy had refused to take in when she agreed to harbour us, and if we could conceal it from Aunt Ivy, a kitten would be a wonderful recompense.

'I'll go up and look,' Squidge said. 'Keep watch for The Dragon, Titch.'

It seemed only a minute before the screams started—Squidge's, a woman's; and then a masculine voice shouting as Squidge fell off the ladder, scrambled to her feet, grabbed my arm and started running. Her face was sickly white and I didn't need her to tell me that something terrible had happened. But what?

It was half an hour before she told me. She'd locked the nursery door behind her as soon as we were inside and no amount of banging and shouting from Aunt Ivy would make her open it. Finally, Aunt Ivy had gone away and that's when Squidge told me. Never, ever again as long as she lived would she fall in love. Men were beasts, animals. She'd never ever forget it. I tried to swallow my impatience. What had she seen? Was it Matthews? What was he doing?

Mother came to fetch us next day and apart from saying that she would explain things when we got home, she barely spoke. She took us up to her bedroom and made Squidge tell her what she'd finally told me—Matthews, with his trousers round his ankles, was on top of Aunt Ivy WHO WAS NAKED. Even worse, he was KISSING her and . . . Squidge couldn't say it aloud to Mother so I had to . . . he was squeezing one of her bosoms.

Poor Mother—sex wasn't something to be talked about, least of all to children. It was something she'd learned AFTER her marriage; so she could not bring herself to tell us that Matthews was having it off with Aunt Ivy. She muttered about Aunt Ivy being married to a much older man who couldn't really be a husband to her. She was lonely, and Matthews was—well, if not a gentleman exactly, he was probably lonely too, and they were just comforting each other. It was wrong of Aunt Ivy, of course—sinful to take off her clothes even if it was a hot day, and the sooner we forgot about it the better. It would be very wrong of us to tell anyone else—even Father; and we must never, ever say a word to poor Uncle Bob. When we were older, she'd be able to explain a little better and we'd understand.

At this point, Mother was beginning to confuse herself as well as us. She drew a deep breath and began again. It was only compassionate to be as understanding as one could in the circumstances and a divorce—well, that would only add to everyone's unhappiness—especially Father's who had an image to maintain, and Uncle Bob was Father's brother. The best thing would be for us to go and unpack and tomorrow we could go with her to visit Father. Wasn't it wonderful that he'd made such a good recovery? It was thought at one time that we might lose him . . . Mother was on safe ground at last . . . Now was there anything—some little surprise—we'd each of us like, to make up for our rather unhappy summer holiday?

Poor Squidge—she'd lost her first love in the cruellest way by finding out that Matthews had never really loved her at all. I felt terribly sorry for her because I could see she was unhappy, but at the same time, I grabbed the chance Mother was offering to make something out of the débâcle.

'Could I have a kitten, Mother? You know how I've always wanted one and it wouldn't be any trouble I promise, and Squidge would like it, too, wouldn't you, Squidge?'

So we got a kitten; and eight years later, Squidge got a wonderful husband and soon after, so did I. Aunt Ivy never invited us to Great Oakmead again and we started having Christmases at home which was much more fun. Poor Uncle Bob only lived a few more years after that summer of 1933 and needless to say, Matthews got the sack. As Mother foretold, we finally did understand. Far from being the ancient old hag we'd thought Aunt Ivy, she was really a pathetic woman, still young and needing what every woman needs, but married to an elderly invalid—and there was Matthews, handsome, sexy, undoubtedly attractive. We thought of him when we read *Lady Chatterley's Lover*!

*   *   *

Arthur and Penny were staring at us open-mouthed.

'What dreadful snobs you were in those days!' was Penny's comment.

Arthur had other things on his mind.

'You're honestly saying you'd no idea those two were having it off?'

'Not a clue!' Squidge said smiling. 'We didn't have sex education in those days,

Arthur.'

'And your mum didn't tell you?'

'It wasn't something you talked about to children.'

'But you must have guessed when you saw people bonking on the telly.'

'We didn't have television in those days, Arthur.'

There was a moment's silence before Arthur stood up and gazed down at us with a pitying smile.

'How utterly boring!' he said, and then looked at me quizzically from beneath his lashes: 'I think you just made all that up, Great Aunt. No one could be THAT innocent could they, Pen? Come on, let's go and have a swim!'

I looked at Squidge as they disappeared in the direction of the pool.

'I said they wouldn't believe it!' Squidge said laughing: then her expression became more thoughtful. 'They see us as deprived!' she said. 'But I'm glad we were so ignorant aren't you, Titch? And it wouldn't have made that much difference to me if I HAD known the truth. What shocked me most was realising that if Matthews wanted to kiss Aunt Ivy, he must prefer her to me!'

'What shocked me was hearing you say you'd seen his hand grasping Aunt Ivy's enormous white bosom!'

We looked at each other and burst out laughing. Despite the incident that long-ago summer, we had shared a wonderfully long, carefree childhood. Now looking back on it, we feel it's today's kids, not us, who are deprived.

9.

Lost
Hope

It was seven o'clock when the thought struck her for the first time that something must be very wrong. It was almost dark and Harry hadn't come home.

Alice put down the iron, a sigh of weariness escaping her as she made her way across the sitting room to the 'phone in the hall. Having sole care of a son of twelve and coping with a full time secretarial job was proving pretty exhausting. With a huge pile of ironing facing her when she'd arrived home this evening, she had been only too glad to agree when Harry asked if he could go and play with the Davis children. It would keep him out from underfoot for a few hours at least.

She dialled the Davis's number. Mrs Davis answered. She sounded worried enough to be slightly incoherent.

'Sean promised he'd have Gillian home by six. He's usually so good about remembering the time. I never do worry when Gilly's with him. They were going to the beech woods adjoining the heath. Len is out looking for them now.'

Alice felt a moment of annoyance. If they were that worried, they might at least have telephoned her, put her in the picture.

As if aware of her thoughts, Meg Davis said:

'We nearly telephoned you to ask if the kids were with you but I knew they couldn't be. You'd have sent my two back long before this, as I told Len.'

Well, that was logical, Alice agreed silently. When Harry did invite the two Davis children for company, she always shooed them off home with a sigh of relief at six o'clock. The flat was tiny and with the three of them rampaging around in it, her nerves couldn't stand any more than a couple of hours. It was different for Meg Davis—she had a huge rambling old house and a husband to read the riot act and keep the children quiet and orderly when required.

Alice put the thought of Brian's absence from her. This was no time to be regretting the absence of Harry's father. A month from now the divorce would be heard in court and that would be the end of her shared life with him.

'Are you still there, Alice? Len's just come in. He says he has shouted himself hoarse and can't see or hear a thing. I'm really worried now.'

Her husband came on the 'phone.

'It's a bit tricky,' he said, sounding calmer than his wife but far from reassuring. 'Meg says the kids could have changed their minds and gone up to the common. I'll go out again with a torch and I'll ring you when I get back.

If they turn up at your place, ring me on my mobile.' He gave her the number.

In the sitting room Alice switched off the television and sat down. Almost at once she stood up again and began to pace up and down the room.

It was absurd to be frightened. The boys—Harry and Sean—were quite old enough to look after themselves, and Gilly, too. It wasn't as if they were little children like the poor Madeleine McCann child. Harry and Sean were twelve, Gilly only a year younger.

'Oh, God!' she whispered. 'Don't let anything have happened to Harry. He's all I've got.'

Now, for the first time since she had walked out and left Brian, she allowed herself to admit the full extent of her loneliness. If it hadn't been for Harry, she might have weakened and returned to Brian. But for her son's sake, she wasn't going to put up with a husband who had no regard whatever for his marriage vows.

She permitted all the old resentment at Brian's act of unfaithfulness to flood through her. She and Harry were better off without a man like that; a father who set such a shocking example to a boy about to enter his teens, a boy who . . .

Harry! She realised that for a few blinding moments, she had forgotten her fear for him. *Why* hadn't the children come home?

Restlessly, she peered out of the window,

half expecting to see Harry's blue-jeaned, grubby figure running towards the block of flats.

I hate this flat, Alice thought irrelevantly. Harry misses the garden. If the children had a garden to play in, they'd never have gone to the woods.

But had they gone to the woods? If not, where else might they be?

Suddenly Alice recalled a remark of Harry's. Only a week or two ago he'd said:

'I told the Davis kids about that really cool tree house I had in the garden where we lived before we came here. Gilly would have loved the rope ladder going up, and coming down on the car tyre.'

Apparently Gillian had asked if he'd show it to her one day and Harry had replied vaguely:

'One day, maybe!'

Could Harry have decided to go to their old home, to catch the bus to Woodland Park, taking the Davis children with him? He might have kept that idea a secret from her, knowing how she felt about his father.

The idea seemed more than possible. Although she and Harry never discussed his father, Alice knew he missed him. Brian wrote, of course, and the boy always grabbed the letters from her and ran to his room with them, stopping whatever he was doing in order to read them without wasting a moment.

For the second time, Alice hurried into the

hall to the 'phone. Thankfully it was Sunday and Brian was at home to answer it.

She explained the reason for her call.

'I just thought . . . well, that they might have gone to visit you,' she ended feebly.

'Well, of course not, Alice. In any case, if they were here I'd have made Harry ring and tell you. Presumably you keep some sort of check on what he's doing?'

Tears, part anger, part disappointment, sprang to Alice's eyes. She brushed them away and said coldly:

'Of course I do! They were in Mrs Davis's charge, not mine. Sorry I bothered you.'

'Look, Al, don't ring off.' His tone of voice had changed, softened. 'You've got *me* worried now. Tell me again what time they were supposed to be back.'

Briefly, she repeated the facts, her own fear increasing as she did so.

'I'll drive over now and help search,' Brian said when she finished her story. 'Chances are they'll be back before I get to you. It'll take me . . . let's see . . . about half an hour. And, Al, if . . . if by any chance they aren't back, then we'll phone the police. They'll soon find them if they haven't got them locked up already!'

Alice walked into the kitchen, found a bottle of wine and poured herself a large glass hoping it would calm her, but it didn't. She did feel relieved that Brian was coming to share her concern but his readiness to do so frightened her. He must think something awful had happened if he felt it necessary to drive over now, at once. At their last unhappy meeting at the solicitor's, they'd resolved never to speak to each other again.

'If you have anything further to say, tell me through my solicitor,' Brian had shouted.

'And that goes for you, too,' she'd shouted back.

Neither of them was thinking of solicitors now.

The well-remembered anger and bitterness returned to her as if it were yesterday. She had never been able to understand how Brian—the one who so violently advocated complete faithfulness in marriage whenever the inevitable topic arose amongst their married friends—should have lowered himself to make love to his teenage typist!

His sordid little affair was degrading—degrading to her, to Harry and to their marriage.

She still felt the same way, despite all her friends' arguments that she was crazy to bust up an otherwise perfectly idyllic marriage over such a trifle.

'But it isn't a trifle to me,' she'd declared. 'Perhaps I'm old fashioned but I believed in my marriage vows and I expected my husband to have meant his, too.'

Her own mother had surprisingly sought to find excuses for Brian. 'My darling Al, we are all human. We all make mistakes. You know he adores you—and the boy. If you really love him, let me remind you that love includes tolerance.'

'Harry's growing up. He tries to emulate his father in everything. I'm not going to have this kind of behaviour set up as an example to him when he's an adult. I've made up my mind. I'm divorcing Brian—for Harry's sake.'

'It's your decision,' her mother had replied. 'Just be quite sure, Al, that it *is* for Harry's good and not to salve your pride. It takes two to make a marriage and two to break one. If Brian has been unfaithful to you, just ask yourself if it could have been your fault.'

Alice poured herself a second glass of wine but left it untouched on the sideboard. She and her mother had never discussed the divorce again. Now, suddenly, Alice knew why. She *was* proud. She had found her mother's suggestion that she might be at fault humiliating. She'd always been a devoted, loving wife to Brian. Their sex life had been satisfactory to them both. She had been blameless. She thought so then and she still thought so.

The 'phone rang suddenly, sending her once more hurrying into the hall.

'Len Davis here, Alice. No sign of them, I'm afraid. I think we should call the police!'

Alice felt momentarily sick. She pulled herself together and said calmly: 'Harry's father will be here soon. Perhaps it would be best to wait until he arrives and we'll both come straight over to your house. We can decide then what's best to do. He'll be here in five minutes or so. Is that all right with you?'

As she resumed her waiting, Alice felt uncertainty pervading her innermost feelings. Would it have been better to call the police at once? If the children were in trouble, then every minute could count and she was being the one to delay assistance.

'Oh, God!' she prayed. 'Don't let me give way. I mustn't cry. Crying won't help them—or me. I'm not going to let Brian see how scared I am. I'll be calm, sensible, do whatever he suggests.'

But when at last she heard him coming up the stairs two at a time, a habit she'd almost forgotten but which instantly identified him to her, she flung open the door of the flat and tears of tension and relief poured down her cheeks.

Brian, after one startled glance at her, put an arm round her shoulders and said:

'Come on, Al. This isn't like you. You've not had . . . bad news, have you?' He looked suddenly frightened, as if until this moment he hadn't believed anything awful had happened to the children.

'No!' she sniffed, feeling calmer and ashamed now of her lack of control. 'There's no news of any kind. Oh, Brian, I'm so scared.

Supposing one of those terrible sex murderers is around? Suppose . . . '

'My dear girl, no sex maniac is going to lure *three* children into his car and assault them. It isn't as if they were *little* kids.'

'But, Brian, there was that terrible case when . . . '

'Stop imagining things, Al. Where's all that cold logic of yours? Can you honestly believe Harry—you know him as well as I do—would just stand by while the two other kids were murdered or assaulted or whatever, calmly awaiting his turn? Of course nothing like that has happened to them. I suppose you realise there's a nasty damp fog creeping up? Amongst the trees the fog could be thick and they might easily have lost their bearings. I'll lay you a pound to a penny that's it.'

Alice relaxed. Hearing Brian's level tone of voice and sensible explanations, her own fears receded to little more than anxiety.

'It is late—nearly nine thirty!' she said. 'If the fog gets worse, they could be out all night!'

Brian was pouring himself some wine. He'd have preferred a whisky, she knew, but she had none. He turned and faced her, his brows drawn down, his face suddenly lined and serious.

'It would probably do Harry a power of good if he had to fend for himself for a week, Al, let alone a night. You've pampered that boy so that he's little better than a sissy. If you don't stop fussing over him he's never going to grow into a man. You've got to let go sometime. You should have started the process years ago and now . . . well, I just hope it's not too late and the boy has guts enough to get himself and the other two out of whatever difficulties they're in.'

Al's mouth had fallen open. She was staring at Brian as if she couldn't credit her own hearing. Never, never had he spoken in this vein to her before. Oh, there'd been the odd scene from time to time. Brian had wanted to pack Harry off to a boarding school, believing that an only child, particularly a boy, needed the company of other boys his own age, a more male environment. They'd compromised on this, with Al promising to see he had more friends home more often; that she wouldn't monopolise Harry's free time because they happened to enjoy each other's company.

There'd been another scene when Brian had wanted to punish Harry for being rude to her. She'd told Brian to keep out of it. She'd punish Harry her own way. Now, trying to search her memory, she could recall other incidents, insignificant seeming at the time, but which had obviously built up into a wall of resentment in Brian; the several occasions when she'd refused to go out somewhere with him because it meant leaving Harry with a baby-sitter.

'The boy's ten!' Brian had stormed. 'This is

absurd, Al. You're treating him like a baby. What about what I want, for a change?'

But Harry has been convalescing from 'flu and she hadn't wanted to leave him just in case he needed her during the evening. Brian's argument that the restaurant was less than a mile away and the baby-sitter had both their mobile telephone numbers had not swayed her.

'Well, let's go round to the Davis's. Perhaps by the time we get there, the kids will have turned up,' Brian interrupted her thoughts.

Sitting beside Brian in his car, Alice remained silent, still deeply shaken by his extraordinary outburst. At last she said:

'I don't accept that what you said just now in the flat was true, but since you obviously thought so, why didn't you speak out at the time?'

Brian glanced down at her and back at the road.

'Where Harry was concerned, you were always right and I was always wrong,' he said, not without bitterness. 'If I'd fought you on every issue I disagreed with over your handling of the boy, we'd have been in the divorce court donkeys' years ago.'

'So you were jealous—jealous of your own son!' Alice cried involuntarily. 'You didn't like it because Harry and I were so close. Now you want to make me feel it was my fault. You're trying to make me feel responsible for what *you* did.'

Brian drew a deep sigh not, as she had expected, replying angrily. He sounded almost weary.

'If I'd wanted to make you feel that way, Al, I'd have said all this at the time we broke up.'

'Then why didn't you?' Alice flared.

'Because I take full responsibility for what I did. It's true that there were many times when I felt excluded by you—not by Harry. He was always pleased to see me, to include me in his games and conversation. You were the one who put Harry first and at times, I felt pretty unhappy. Not jealous, Al, unhappy. But I don't offer that as an excuse.'

For the second time that evening, Alice remembered her mother's words.

'It takes two to make a marriage, Alice, and two to break one. Just ask yourself if it could have been your fault.'

'You should have told me how you felt, Brian!'

'Would it have made any difference?'

No! she thought. No, he's right. I wouldn't have listened. Why am I listening now? Because of Harry? Because . . .

'Brian, you don't honestly think anything terrible has happened, do you?'

'If you really mean "honestly", then I don't know. But I do know we're going to do everything possible to find him.'

Five hours later, Alice gave up hope.

'They'll find them in the morning,' Brian said as she cried against his chest. 'Now it's after three. You must try to get some rest.'

The police had been out in numbers since eleven o'clock searching the woods and the surrounding heath. The fog had closed down completely and at two-thirty the search had been called off until daylight. Meg Davis had had hysterics and been given sedatives by her doctor. Len Davis, like Brian, had been out helping the searchers and was exhausted. Alice herself, whose pride sustained her all through those hours waiting at the Davis's house, was now at her lowest ebb.

'He's dead! I know it! I know I'll never see him alive again. I think he's drowned, Brian—in that horrible lake in the wood. It's thirty feet deep in the middle. Harry told me.'

Brian wiped the tears from her cheeks and tilted her chin so that she was forced to look straight into his eyes.

'Harry can swim!' he said slowly. 'So can the other two—Mrs Davis said so. Even if one jumped in to help another there'd still be a third to go for help. No, Al, Harry hasn't drowned. That much I am sure of. Show me some of that courage of yours.' He actually managed a smile. 'You're a fine one,' he said gently. 'I try to cheer you up and you just start crying again.'

'I know, I know!' she sobbed. 'I was just remembering—the only time you ever did overrule me with Harry was when you insisted he learned to swim. I thought he was too young and you said . . . '

Suddenly, Brian's arms were tightening round her. She could feel his heart thudding against her forehead.

'Oh, Al, if you can think that way, don't you realise there's hope—for us, I mean? Don't you see, darling, that if you can admit I might have been right about Harry in one respect, I could have been right about other aspects of his upbringing, too? I think it's right that you should love Harry—I love him, too—and wonderful that you should be so close to the boy. But you were becoming mother *and* father. I should have been strong and stuck up for my paternal rights from the very beginning. Instead, I was weak. I let you have your own way. Trouble is, I always have been weak where you were concerned. I loved you so much. I still do. I wanted you to be happy and for our marriage to be free from rows and scenes. So I sat back . . . '

'Oh, Brian!' Alice cried. 'I never realised!'

'I know you probably can't understand why . . . why I had that silly affair with Linda. For a little while she made me feel important—a man again. She really looked up to me and let me believe my opinions counted. It was a form of conceit, I suppose, I needed someone to bolster my self-confidence. If you'd needed me, you . . . '

'Brian, I did need you. I do! I've been utterly miserable. A dozen times I've regretted our separation, but I was too proud to admit it even to myself. I've been a fool, an utter fool!'

Once again, Brian was smiling.

'Come on now, less of that self-abasement. It isn't like my Al. The trouble with you is, you're worn out. I'm going to put you to bed.'

'No!' she said, clinging to him. 'I can't sleep.'

'Then we'll stay here and sit it out together,' Brian said firmly. He lifted her up and carried her over to the settee. He took off her jacket and shoes and made her stretch out full length, tucking a cushion in behind her head.

'Now relax. I'm going to make us both a hot drink.'

She closed her eyes and tried, wearily, to sort out her conflicting emotions. If it were not for her fears for Harry she could be happy—so very, very happy. She and Brian were together again. She knew now that the divorce would never come to court. Perhaps there would be a new start to their new life together.

A start without Harry?

No, it was unthinkable! Brian had all but proved to her nothing terrible could have happened . . . not to the three of them together. It was only the fog which had made them lose their way. In the morning when the fog cleared, they would be found . . . safe . . . alive. Perhaps even a little pleased with themselves at having such an adventure.

She heard Brian come back into the room; felt the sofa give a little as he sat down beside her. She was very, very frightened; and very, very tired. Brian's lips brushed against her cheek.

'Go to sleep, darling. He'll be all right.'

She slipped her hand into his and together they began their long wait for the dawn.

10.

The Sapphire Ring
Transience

Naomi looked up from her sewing machine as her granddaughter Cathy came hurrying into the room, her pretty face glowing, her blue eyes sparkling. She gave her grandmother a quick kiss and then thrust her arm in front of Naomi's face.

'Look!' she said breathlessly. 'Pete gave it to me. We've got engaged. Isn't it beautiful?'

Naomi forced a smile to hide her dismay.

'It's the same colour as the dress I'm wearing at the party tomorrow,' Cathy announced as she studied the sparkling sapphire ring on her finger. 'Is my dress nearly finished?'

Naomi, a skilled seamstress, was copying a dress Cathy had seen on Neighbours, worn by that girl called Summa who was Cathy's current idol. She nodded.

'It's nearly ready for you to try on. Meanwhile, can you lay the table, darling? You'll have to empty the dishwasher first.'

Domestic chores were not Cathy's favourite pastime but this evening she was obviously on cloud nine and willing to do anything. She hummed happily as she laid out knives and forks. Naomi started pinning up the hem of her granddaughter's dress.

'Does this mean you've broken up with Andrew?' she asked, keeping her voice as casual as possible.

Cathy nodded.

'Uh-huh! I always fancied Pete best but he was engaged to Annabel.'

'So Andrew was second best!' Naomi said with a sigh. 'That was a bit unkind, wasn't it? So how long do you plan to stay engaged to Pete?'

Cathy put down the butter dish she was holding and gazed dreamily at her sapphire ring.

'Until we get married, of course.'

Naomi caught her breath. Ever since the child's parents had divorced, she had looked after their only daughter and she preferred not to think of the day when Cathy would leave home. Even though Pete might well get dumped like Andrew, her granddaughter was so pretty, she would never lack for suitors. Then Naomi's spirits rose as she reminded herself of the characters in the T.V. soap whom Pete and Cathy were probably emulating.

As it happened, she liked young Pete— preferred him to Cathy's former love, Andrew. According to Cathy, he was not only clever but all the girls in her class fancied him. Doubtless it was a feather in Cathy's cap to be the 'chosen one'! These boy/girl relationships were very different from the way things were in her young days. Not only did they not start 'courting' until they'd left school, but getting engaged was a fairly momentous occasion and engagements were rarely broken.

Naomi sighed as she took the remaining pins out of her mouth and turned to her granddaughter.

'Only the hem to sew now, darling,' she said. 'We'll have tea first and then you can try the dress on.'

Cathy hurried over and gave her an excited hug as she put the ring against the material.

'See, it matches exactly!' she said, planting a kiss on her grandmother's cheek. 'I'm going to have a blue dress just like this for my wedding.'

For a tiny moment, Naomi's heart missed a beat, and then she let out her breath and smiled.

Why in the name of goodness was she fussing about a sapphire ring which almost certainly came out of a cracker? And as for her granddaughter's wedding, it would not be for many years yet since Cathy was only eight.

11.

Christmas Spirit
Charity

He glanced at his watch and saw that it was nearly five-thirty. Any moment now the shop would close and he'd be too late. The palms of his hands were damp and he could feel his heart thumping so loudly in his chest that he feared the people milling round him must surely hear it. He'd been wandering round the store for over an hour trying to get up courage to carry out his intent. Time was fast running out and he could not delay any longer.

Glancing quickly to his left and right, he drew a deep breath and reached up to the shelf above him. Too frightened now to check whether he had been observed, he stuffed the article into his tartan shopping trolley. Every instinct was warning him to get out now . . . quickly, before he was arrested; but his feet seemed rooted to the ground. Breathing deeply, he tried to retain control of his panic. Thief! Thief! For the first time in eighty years, he was stealing something that was not his. His guilt was overwhelming—yet he knew he must go through with his plan. There was something else he must take before he could get out of the shop and make his way to the safety of his home.

A woman barged into him, knocking his elbow with her wire basket.

'Sorry!' she muttered, staring at him for a brief moment. Was it in apology or had she seen him putting the cardboard box in his trolley?

Once again, guilt engulfed him; but the woman had turned away and he realised that for the moment anyway, he was safe.

Slowly, the ability to move his legs returned. Head down, he edged his way past other customers engrossed in their Christmas shopping, to the adjoining shelves. He'd come to the shop every day for the past week and knew exactly what he wanted; where to locate them; how impossibly expensive they were; how totally beyond his or Debbie's means.

Furtively, he glanced around him. There seemed to be fewer people now and his sense of danger increased. There must be no more hesitation. He'd done it once—he could do it again . . .

Three minutes later, he was standing in the queue at the check-out, waiting to be charged for a Christmas card and two strands of tinsel—legitimate purchases for which he would pay. It was part of his carefully thought-out plan. One more minute and he'd be safely away . . .

Suddenly, he knew that he couldn't go through with it. He'd thought he would be strong enough just once to go against the very

85

principles by which he had lived—fair play, integrity and honesty. He would have to turn around and put the precious objects back.

*　　　*　　　*

Mary Saunders was tired. Even on ordinary days, a store detective's job meant being constantly on your feet but on the day before Christmas, the store was crowded and she was exhausted. For it to happen now, just before closing time . . . Her warm brown eyes regarded the old man with a mixture of irritation and compassion.

'Since you have admitted you intended to steal the goods, sir, I'm afraid you'll have to come with me to see the manager. I'm not in a position to let you go.'

'I was going to put them back, truly I was. If that poor woman hadn't fallen over.'

He said the same thing to the manager as he sat facing him in his small private office.

'You see, I've never stolen anything in my life; but Debbie—my daughter—her husband left her and the children and it's all she can do to manage.' He stared down at the colourful Barbie doll smiling through the cellophane of her cardboard box. 'It's the one thing my little granddaughter wanted so badly—last Christmas, her birthday and now . . . I tried to save enough but . . . and then there was Action Man for young Tim. Debbie and I between us thought we might have enough but last week my pension money was stolen so . . . so I couldn't bear to think of the children waking up in the morning and finding Father Christmas had forgotten them again. So I thought—you have so many toys on the shelves it wouldn't make that much difference if . . . but of course, that's not the point, is it? It would have been stealing.'

'Indeed it would!' The manager's voice was sharp as he eyed the old pensioner. Nearly every shoplifter had a sob story to tell. This sounded like the truth.

'What do you think, Miss Saunders?' he asked.

'A woman customer in the queue at the till fell over!' she said quietly. 'If this gentleman hadn't turned to help her up, he could have gone through the till and I wouldn't have spotted the toys in his trolley . . . and it is Christmas, sir.'

The manager nodded, his eyes thoughtful. Then he said:

'You can put those boxes back on the shelves, Miss Saunders; and when you've done that, you might pop along to the store room—I think you might find something appropriate for this customer's grandchildren among the "spoiled items". I'm fairly sure I saw a Barbie doll in a damaged carton. See what you can find.'

The children were in bed and he sat with Debbie at the kitchen table as she wrapped up the parcels ready for the morning.

'So the police weren't called in after all!' she said as he finished his story. 'Really, Dad, I know you meant it for the best but just think what we'd have felt like if you'd had to go to prison! I know you love the kids—and they love you, but . . . well, promise me you'll never even think of such a thing again! Having got that off my chest, I can't believe that manager let you have all these toys for free after what you nearly did! It's his job to sell things—not give them away. Whatever can have got into him?'

'Kindness, perhaps, charity, benevolence, compassion . . . ' He paused, glancing at the children's drawings of the nativity scene proudly displayed on the door of the fridge, and smiled: 'Whatever his motives, Debbie, I think you'll agree, they all add up to a very generous helping of Christmas spirit.'

12.

The Tradition
Indecision

At first when the snow fell in swift small streaks, sharp and hard against the windscreen, he'd thought it was hail, but gradually it turned to large soft white flakes, drifting slowly into the headlights as if drawn by magnets towards the car. It piled up on either side of the wipers and on the window edges, obscuring vision and giving the two occupants the sensation of slow suffocation.

'Damnation! Can't see a thing!'

Neil's voice was loud in the silence surrounding them and Roz could clearly distinguish the angry impatience behind his controlled tone of voice.

'Oh, well,' she said, her own voice sounding brittle and false, 'at least it looks like being a white Christmas!'

'My dear Roz, who wants a white Christmas? Of all the ridiculous remarks! Do you realize we've over a hundred and fifty miles to go? We'll never make it in this.'

She sighed. Nowadays it seemed as if they couldn't talk to each other without coming to grief, ending with bitter, hurtful remarks each trying to outdo the other until there was a

89

blazing row, a parting, a day or two of silence and then a drifting together once more. What was wrong with them? What had happened to them?

The desolation of the empty darkness outside the car found an echo in her soul. Something was frozen tightly within her; she couldn't any longer reveal her thoughts to Neil. She could only make more stupid remarks and provoke yet another row. If she cried—and oh, how she wished she could cry—would they be frozen tears? Could a frozen person cry snow?

'Does it matter so very much if we don't get there tonight?' she asked in a softer, conciliatory tone. 'After all, you didn't tell your parents when we were arriving. They won't worry if we don't show up. We could stop at the next hotel and perhaps by morning . . .'

'Look, Roz, I'm sure you're trying to be helpful but you don't understand,' Neil broke in sharply. 'They *will* worry. I suppose it sounds silly to you but even though I didn't actually tell them when I'd be coming, they'll expect us tonight. I *always* go home on Christmas Eve.'

Neil cast a swift sideways glance at the girl beside him: tall, slim, blonde, beautiful Roz, his girl. He had fallen instantly head-over-heels in love with her when they'd met at Tom's party, knowing that this was the one girl in the world he wanted to marry. In the weeks and months that followed, he had fallen deeper and deeper in love; Neil Thurloe who had vowed to stay a bachelor not just for the remaining half of his twenties but for life. Miraculously, Roz had fallen for him too. What a fantastic, unbelievable, golden, glorious summer it had been!

It had started to go wrong when he had asked her to marry him and she had said 'no'.

'I love you, Neil, but I utterly refuse to rush into marriage' she said. 'My own parents were divorced when I was just a kid and I never had a settled home. I have to be sure—totally sure—before I commit myself and I want you to be sure, too. It may sound old-fashioned but for me, marriage means once only. If we're not right for each other, now is the time for us to find out.'

At first he'd laughed. It had seemed so absurd when they were obviously so totally 'right for each other'.

'Darling, we can't be *sure*. Please don't rush me.'

He'd tried to play the game her way, give her the time she wanted. In every other way the summer they spent almost exclusively in each other's company was idyllic.

'We've known each other six months,' he said when the first golden leaves started to fall and the air in London's parks cooled a little and brought to them a whisper of autumn. 'I want you to come home to Devon with me,

Roz—meet my parents. Mother's last letter said she was beginning to doubt you really existed!'

Her fingers lay warm and brown, curled inside his palm. He felt their tightening.

'Darling, not just yet. Meeting your parents—well, it's an old-fashioned preliminary to getting engaged. Isn't it?'

'Well, aren't we as good as engaged? And what's wrong with being engaged, come to that? Everyone knows you're my girl.'

'Your parents don't!' Roz replied. 'You've said they are old-fashioned; that they wouldn't approve of trial marriages. We might let something slip—some little thing I might say about you fixing the washer in our kitchen or that our bedroom wallpaper has started peeling. I know how very much you love them Neil and I don't want to risk their disapproval.'

He found Roz's conflicting attitudes confusing. She was so modern in every way. It was she who had suggested she go to live with him, share his flat; who thought trial marriages were a sensible safeguard against marrying the wrong person.

He didn't understand the paradoxes in her nature, and now he found himself wondering if her real reason for refusing to meet his elderly parents was because she knew she'd be bored to tears by them, or because, as she'd so often told him, she thought Christmas was no longer the joyful family occasion it used to be and had become so commercialized, it had lost its meaning.

The snow was falling steadily now and the black road in front of him had turned white. His speed was down to a little under thirty and he reckoned that, even supposing the snow let up, they wouldn't get home till after ten. At least that would be in plenty of time for the midnight service . . .

'You intended to go home for Christmas whether I agreed to go with you or not, didn't you, Neil? You wouldn't have stayed in London with me.'

Roz's voice sounded cold, accusing. He felt trapped, put on the defensive.

'All right, I admit it. I've never *not* gone home for Christmas if I could possibly make it. You don't understand what it means to my parents, Roz. It's the one time of the year they can be absolutely sure they'll have me home.'

For a moment, she didn't answer. When she spoke her voice was sharper as she pursued the same subject.

'You deliberately let me think you were waiting for me to make up my mind before you decided to go home.'

'So what if I did? Has it occurred to you I was doing it for your sake? I didn't want you to feel you HAD to come. I wanted you to choose to come of your own accord; for it to be your wish as well as mine.'

'I don't see what difference that makes.

What if I'd said no? You'd have driven off this afternoon and left me alone in the flat over Christmas? Was that the idea?'

'No, it wasn't!' he burst out, now furious with her. 'That's exactly the kind of blackmail I was trying to avoid. If you'd *known* I meant to go anyway, you'd probably have opted to come with me rather than spend Christmas on your own. I wanted you *to want* to come!'

In one way, Roz could understand his reasoning. In another, she was desperately hurt. It wasn't so much that Neil had, in a sense, cheated her, tricked her, as that he could ever have contemplated leaving her alone over Christmas—the four uninterrupted days they had both so much looked forward to. Not that they had made any special preparations. Roz didn't believe in tinsel and trees and holly and mistletoe. They belonged far, far back with childhood, to the days before her parents had divorced.

'I think it would have been about the most cruel thing you could have done—going off and leaving me in the flat alone!' she spoke her thoughts aloud.

'Oh, for God's sake!' Neil said bitterly. 'I didn't do it, did I? Why all the fuss about what might have happened? Maybe I knew all along you'd come with me.'

'You couldn't have known. I didn't know myself until this morning when suddenly I thought I ought to come because it mattered so much to you . . . or it seemed to matter so much. I'm beginning to wonder now if I made the right decision. Maybe I should have let you go alone. Maybe I've been making a lot of wrong decisions lately and you and I . . . '

Her words, becoming every second a little more hysterical, came to an abrupt halt as the car skidded across the road, scraped a hidden kerb and slowly righted itself.

'Have to slow up a bit,' Neil said matter-of-factly. 'I'd crept up over thirty and it won't do in these conditions.'

She felt shaken, not just because of the near-accident but by her own outburst. She hadn't meant to say so much but now that she had actually voiced the words, they wouldn't leave her mind. Perhaps he really didn't want her with him. Perhaps, as she had feared, Neil was just infatuated, physically attracted. Perhaps it had not been love—real love—for either of them after all.

She leant back against the car seat and closed her eyes.

She was so tired, tired of worrying, tired of fighting but most of all, tired of the not knowing. She was sure of only one thing—that she could not bear to marry the wrong man the way her parents had married each other. She could not bear it if all the loving sweetness that she and Neil had shared ever turned to bitterness, to hate. She would rather lose him now.

Roz shivered, not so much from the cold as from fear. Their relationship seemed to be getting out of control and they were starting to quarrel all the time.

As if deliberately to accentuate her fears, Neil said:

'I expect you'll be terribly bored. My parents are pretty square, I suppose, and as I told you, Christmas for them is totally traditional. I can see now I was stupid to think you might like the set-up.'

'You may be right,' Roz said coldly.

The snow now lessened and Neil was able to increase his speed to around forty. Neither of them spoke until they were barely an hour's drive from Neil's home when he said abruptly:

'I'd appreciate it if you'd put up a pretence. My parents . . . well, it would be distressing for them if they thought we weren't . . . '

'I quite understand!' Roz broke in, biting her lip in the darkness. 'I'm quite capable of playing the part of adoring girlfriend, if that's what you mean.'

'Yes, that's exactly what I mean,' Neil said, suddenly furiously angry with her. Somehow she had forced him into apologizing for his parents, his home. She'd spoilt this Christmas in some strange, unfathomable, feminine way, putting him in the wrong just as if he had forced her to come with him against her will.

They drove in total silence. Beside him, Roz's thoughts were racing in circles. If I were to tell him I was going to have his child . . . but I don't want him to be loving just because . . . then I'd never know . . . that's the whole purpose in *not* telling him. I'll have to tell him soon . . . that is, if I'm going to tell him at all. Maybe I would have told him if it hadn't been for his remark . . . funny how it stuck in my mind . . . *'Divorce is all right if there aren't any children, but a child, in my view, makes all the difference. A child needs a father as well as a mother. I'd always put the child's interests before my own . . .'*

Oh, yes, Roz told herself miserably, Neil would do the right thing and offer to marry her at once and probably try to insist on her marrying him no matter how she felt about it. Then she'd never know . . . never know if he really loved her. Funny what a conventional person he was at heart beneath the modern jargon and veneer. It had taken quite a time to discover that it *was* only a veneer. Soon she'd *have* to tell him . . . or leave him. Maybe this weekend would finish everything between them anyway. She'd be bound not to fit in at his home—he'd all but said so. There'd be a blazing row on the drive back to town and that would be that. Maybe it was best this way. Maybe . . .

'We're here!' Neil said before she realized the car had come to a halt. They were parked outside a flint stone cottage, each small oblong window ablaze with light. The front door opened and a short grey-haired woman came into the square of orange light and called to them.

'Neil, is that you, dear? Your father and I were so worried with all the snow. Father said you'd make it somehow, but I couldn't help worrying just in case . . .'

The three of them moved into the little hall. Neil's father—an elderly, balding edition of Neil—came from another room to greet them.

'You must be Roz—and a frozzed Roz, I'll be bound!' he laughed at his joke, shook Roz warmly by the hand and pulled her into the sitting room where a huge Yule log spluttered and sparked in the fireplace.

Roz glanced round her, not quite sure whether to laugh or cry. Conventional Christmas was hardly an adequate description. A tree, ablaze with fairy lights and tinsel, topped by a white crêpe paper angel, stood by the window. Round every picture, red-berried holly had been twisted to form a frame. The mantelshelf was covered with Christmas cards depicting angels, robins and merry gentlemen and more cards sat propped on the bookcase and each table-top. To complete the effect, a nativity scene of cut-out cardboard figures standing on a layer of straw, and flanked on either side by candles, had been carefully arranged on an oak chest beside the tree.

'It's all very pretty, isn't it, Neil?' she said, trying to keep to her side of their agreement.

98

'You must have gone to a lot of trouble, Mrs Thurloe.'

'Oh, it was no trouble, dear. I enjoy it. In fact, I look forward to Christmas for months beforehand.'

The blue eyes smiled warmly into Roz's. Roz felt a sudden anxiety that her words might have sounded patronizing. She hadn't meant them to be.

'You'll be coming to the midnight service?' Mr Thurloe asked, addressing his son as well as Roz.

'Yes, of course,' Neil said quickly.

'Well, Roz isn't going!' Mrs Thurloe announced before Roz herself could speak. 'I never saw anyone look so tired.'

'But we always go . . . ' Neil began, his eyes fastened on Roz as if willing her to agree with him that she *would* go, as if her attendance was a matter of life or death. But Mrs Thurloe interrupted him.

'I'm a great believer in holding to the traditions as well you know, Neil, but I'll not have them followed to the point of stupidity. This poor girl is exhausted, and I can see it even if you can't.' She put an arm round Roz's shoulders. 'It's into bed with you, my dear, and right away.'

Roz's feeble protests were over-ruled. Mrs Thurloe led her upstairs to a spotlessly clean, white bedroom, where a fire burned in the little black grate, casting shadows and a glow

99

over the multi-coloured, patchwork bedspread.

'How lovely!' For the first time, Roz was able to be totally sincere. 'How kind of you to go to so much trouble—a fire.'

She was suddenly reminded of her indecision this morning. She might so easily have said 'No!' to Neil and then this kind woman would have prepared her room, lit the fire, for nothing.

'You can have a bath in the morning,' Mrs Thurloe said. 'There are two hot water bottles in the bed. You pop straight in, my dear, and I'll bring you up something to eat.'

Suddenly Roz felt the full extent of her tiredness. She was more than content to let Neil's mother order her about, take charge. The tension in her nerves was easing and her whole body drooped with a terrible fatigue. She undressed, washed and fell into bed, cuddling one hot water bottle and wrapping her frozen feet around the other. Warmth pervaded her and she thought drowsily; patchwork bedspreads are supposed to be old-fashioned but they're really very mod. Psychedelic, in fact!

'There now, dear, I've brought you some soup. And just to make you smile, I've put it in The Soup Plate!'

She sat down on the edge of the bed and put an odd-shaped bowl on Roz's lap. Her blue eyes twinkled.

'It's really a large shaving bowl!' she

explained. 'Hence the covered half, for the brush, and the opening, for the water. Neil gave it to me one Christmas when he was only a little boy. He'd saved up for it for weeks so none of us had the heart to tell him his Soup Plate was really a shaving bowl. Since then, we've always used it for soup whenever anyone's ill in bed. It doesn't spill as easily as an open plate.'

'I'm not really very hungry,' Roz said, but to please her hostess, she drank a little. It was so appetizing, she finished it all.

'When you and Neil are married, you shall have this bowl,' Mrs Thurloe announced, taking it from her. 'It'll be useful for your children when they go through the mumps and measles stage.'

Roz lay back against the pillows, the tension mounting once more inside her. If she'd known how charming and kind and trusting this woman would turn out to be, she'd never have made that promise to Neil to pretend for the weekend. It seemed all wrong to let his mother believe she and Neil were going to be married. Straightforward honesty was one of her most rigid principles. She couldn't deceive this woman.

Words came tumbling out in incoherent distress.

' . . . Not sure if we *should* get married . . . not sure if it's the real thing for Neil . . . my own parents *thought* they were in love . . . and anyway, how does one know? I am sure I love Neil but . . . '

'My dear child, if that's all that is worrying you—why, I can put your mind and heart at rest at once. Of course Neil loves you. He wouldn't have brought you home otherwise.'

Roz's heart, which had leapt momentarily when it seemed she had the proof she so desperately sought, sank back into despair.

'You don't understand, Mrs Thurloe. Neil asked me down because he didn't want to leave me alone in London over Christmas. He knew I'd hate being without him. It was just kindness on his part, don't you see?'

Mrs Thurloe drew a deep breath.

'So Neil hasn't told you about our Christmas tradition?'

'Well, he told me you kept Christmas in the old-fashioned way—midnight service on Christmas Eve, the exchanging of presents on Christmas morning, the Queen's speech after lunch and afterward the tree presents.'

'But he didn't tell you about the brides!' Mrs Thurloe said smiling. 'So I'll tell you myself. We don't know exactly how far back in history the habit began but all the Thurloes are brought up, generation after generation, to look upon Christmas as a Family Day. Perhaps it isn't really very Christian-minded, but the day is kept for the family only. No friends not even boyfriends or girlfriends—just *family*. The only time anyone spends Christmas at home who isn't a Thurloe is when the son or daughter brings home the girl or boy they love and intend to marry.'

Mrs Thurloe watched Roz's face as she absorbed the words and then, slowly, the meaning.

'It's surprising, really, that a silly old family tradition like that should have survived so long and yet, do you know, Roz, it's amazing how well it all seems to work out. Somehow it seems to have made all the youngsters hesitate before they've plunged into matrimony; stop, and think twice whether they're sure the person they love really will make the right wife or husband. Why, the first year I met Neil's father, he never did invite me home for Christmas. I knew about the tradition and it nearly broke my heart. I was sure he didn't love me. But the next year . . . well, he'd finished taking his law exams and he was more settled in himself then about his future. That second Christmas he did ask me. The extra year of waiting gave him the time he needed to grow up. I didn't realize it at the time but afterwards I often thought how the Thurloe tradition might have been the making of our marriage. So you see, dear, you don't have to doubt Neil. *He's* sure. All you have to know now is how *you* feel. Now, no more talking. What you need more than anything if you're to enjoy tomorrow, is sleep.'

At that moment, as the door closed behind

Neil's mother, Roz knew that sleep was impossible. She had far too much to think about. The next moment, unaccountably, she was asleep.

She awoke several hours later. The fire had died down to a glimmer but still cast enough light for her to see her watch. Nearly two a.m. The house was deathly quiet, as if holding its breath. Neil and his parents must have returned from the midnight service and be asleep.

Suddenly, Roz was terribly wide awake. She felt tense and utterly unable to relax back into sleep. She swung her legs to the floor and slipped on her dressing gown. Without quite knowing why, she tiptoed out of her room and, fumbling a little in the strangeness of the house, found her way downstairs.

The Yule log in the sitting room glowed warm and welcoming. Roz stood in front of it for a moment, gathering in its heat. Then she turned and walked over to the tree. Fairy lights, tinsel, glass balls, and now, added to it, a circle of brightly-wrapped parcels. The label on one of them was clearly addressed 'For Roz'. From Neil? From his parents? What was in it? Curiosity worked in her. She felt the shape of the package trying to guess. Suddenly she was back in her very early childhood doing exactly the same thing. Father had come downstairs and found her and sent her back to her room, but not angrily. Then Mother had come and tucked her back into bed. It was the first time in her life she had been actively aware she was happy.

'Dear God,' she had prayed with childish faith, 'let me go on being as happy as this for ever and ever and I'll be good for ever and ever, Amen!'

But the 'ever and ever' had lasted one half year; then the divorce. The following Christmas had been spent at school; subsequent ones alternately with her mother or her father, who now lived apart, Father at his club and Mother in a small London flat. At the club it was merely a turkey lunch. In the flat, her mother saying 'I don't think we'll bother with holly, it's so messy!' And two years later: 'Do you really want a tree, Roz? Let's use the money we save to go to a really good show.'

'Roz! I thought you were in bed, asleep.'

She turned at the sound of Neil's voice, unaware that the tears were pouring down her cheeks. She stood completely immobile, the package in her hands, staring at him. He came across the room and took her in his arms.

'Darling, you're crying. Why? Not on Christmas Eve! Look, if you're unhappy, I'll drive you back to London. Now, tonight . . . this morning. Why . . . ' he smiled down at her, ' . . . why it's Christmas Day.'

Suddenly, her whole body seemed to soften, to melt and to liquefy in one golden stream of love for him. Where there had been confusion, fear, loneliness, suddenly there was joy and happiness, a happiness as real, as tangible as that Christmas Eve so many years ago.

'I love you!' she said, and knew the words were perfectly, completely true. 'I love you, Neil.'

He smiled down at her, and gently touched the package she still clasped in her hands. 'Perhaps this will prove how much I love you,' he said softly. 'We'll break the old Thurloe tradition if you want, darling. You can open your present now if you like. After all, it is Christmas Day.'

'But you never have tree presents until after the Queen's speech!' Roz cried without thinking.

'So what?' Neil laughed. 'Open it now and we'll wrap it up again. Who cares about old-fashioned traditions?'

'I do!' Roz whispered, and, very carefully, replaced her present beneath the tree.

13.

The Chain
Fear

It was a cold January day, and through the rough circle of glass I had cleared on the train window, I could see the dark clouds, heavy with the snow the radio had forecast. The trees bordering the ploughed fields were leafless, their bare limbs sticking out like gaunt, ghostly arms against the dark grey sky.

I turned my gaze back to the only other occupant of the compartment—a middle-aged, grey-haired woman with a thin, lined face. She struck me as someone who had suffered in her life—was still suffering, perhaps. Was it from a physical ailment? Perhaps she had recently been bereaved . . .

Poor soul, I thought, suddenly tremendously glad that I was young, healthy, with my whole life before me. In two hours' time, I'd be reunited with Martin. I had not seen him for three whole days—the longest we'd ever been apart since our marriage last June. My sister had had a baby and I had been down to London to see her and my new niece. But much as I loved Janey, I couldn't wait to be back with Martin—my husband. Those words still sounded strange, and wonderful. I loved him so much! Even to think about him made me restless, anxious for this journey to be over quickly.

I picked up my paper and found the crossword. It was not particularly difficult but I badly needed one word to help me finish it. *'Connected course or train of events'*, was the five-letter clue. I chewed the end of my biro but remained defeated.

'Perhaps I can help? I'm quite good at crosswords!'

My travelling companion was smiling now, the face transformed from its former sadness. I returned her smile and read out the clue.

'Could it be "chain"?' she suggested.

'Of course! Links!' I agreed, filling in the letters. When I looked up, I saw her staring at the label on the overnight bag I'd put on the luggage rack.

The smile had left my companion's face as she leaned forward and stared into my eyes. It was as if she was trying to look right into me, I thought then. Now I know she was doing exactly that, but at the time, I didn't question her curiosity because, quite suddenly, she said:'Do you believe in ghosts?'

'In ghosts? No, I don't! I think people who profess to have seen one have over-active imaginations.'

Realising suddenly that my truthful answer might offend this woman who, for all I knew, could believe in the manifestation of the supernatural, I added quickly: 'Of course, I could be wrong.'

'I believe in a spirit world; that there are unhappy spirits who can haunt us.'

Her voice was so matter-of-fact, so unmelodramatic that, extraordinary though this conversation was, it didn't seem in any way macabre. In any event, a debate on such a subject with someone I'd never see again was a welcome diversion that could help to pass the time now I had finished my crossword.

'I'm afraid I don't believe in haunted houses either!' I said with a smile. 'Have you ever been in one, Mrs ...?'

'Mrs Bramley, Kitty Bramley!' she filled in for me.

'And my name is Kate,' I introduced myself.

There was a long pause whilst she stared at me intently and then she said abruptly:

'Yes, I saw your name on your luggage strap. No, I've never been in a haunted house but I am visited by a ghost.'

The matter-of-fact tone of Mrs Bramley's voice belied the melodramatic words. I was overcome by curiosity.

'Won't you tell me about it? I'm really intrigued!' I said. 'I want to be a writer, and what you've just said fires my imagination. My real name is Katherine, by the way, although Martin, my husband, and my family and friends all call me Kate.'

'Aaah!' The long-drawn out exclamation was accompanied by a violent nodding of Mrs

Bramley's head.

'That's the link, you see.' Seeing my look of incomprehension, she added: 'Kitty is an abbreviation of Katherine, just as Kate is. We are linked by the name we share; but for your sake, my dear, I don't think I should tell you my story, especially not as you want to be an author.'

'You mean, I might tell other people! Well, I won't—you have my word. In any case, I could change names and places so that no one would ever connect the story with you.'

'My dear girl, I am not concerned about the connection.'

There was another long pause during which I held my breath. Her very reluctance to unburden herself was only adding to my curiosity.

I had to wait until the train had restarted after a brief stop at a station where mercifully no one entered our compartment, before she spoke, her voice a low monotone as she began her story. It was wartime, she related, and the Germans were sending massive waves of bombers to pulverise London in what Mrs Bramley called 'the Blitzkrieg'. Although thousands of children had been evacuated, many parents had allowed them to return home during the 'phoney war' when the enemy was still busy invading the rest of Europe. When the bombing did start, hundreds of people were made homeless. Places had to be found quickly for orphaned children, and for those temporarily without a parent or relative. Mrs Bramley's Aunt Kay, then twenty years old, had gone to help in one of the temporary refuges.

'When she first went to work there, she was put in charge of one particular casualty, a young woman whose daughter had gone missing when their house had been bombed. An air-raid warden had found her frantically searching for her child. She had no physical injuries but was clearly traumatised as she was completely withdrawn and never spoke.'

Mrs Bramley drew a long sigh.

'Kay said it was desperately sad to see her despair when new casualties were brought in but did not include her daughter.'

'That's really sad!' I said. 'What happened to her?'

'At first, nothing, but every day and most nights, the raids continued and room had to be found for more of the homeless. One day, a dear little girl of about two years old was brought in. The following afternoon, Aunt Kay was on duty when she came upon the young woman sitting by the cot. As my aunt approached, she looked straight at her and said: "My daughter's sleeping." Of course, Aunt Kay knew it wasn't her daughter but she had started talking so they left her by the child.'

The smile on Mrs Bramley's face faded and

was replaced by that same look of sadness I'd noticed earlier. She turned to gaze out of the window and when next she looked at me, she seemed to be in a waking dream.

'For the next three weeks, the young mother was seldom far from the toddler's side. She still wouldn't talk to any of the staff or to the other occupants but she started to sing nursery rhymes to the child; and although she talked endlessly to her, she stopped immediately anyone approached. The doctors were convinced it would not be long before she decided to speak normally. Then, one night, after a particularly bad raid, an incendiary bomb set fire to the roof. No one was hurt but the top floor was too badly damaged to be used and the residents were dispersed elsewhere. As a result the woman and the toddler were separated.'

Mrs Bramley's figure slumped against the back of the seat. I had to lean forward to hear her voice as she said in a whisper:

'My aunt had been given two days' leave— to buy her wedding dress, actually. When she went back to work, Matron asked her to see if there was anything she could do to distract the young mother. You see, in her distressed state she had been convinced the child was her own missing daughter, whereas the toddler had been reunited with its real mother. When the woman saw Aunt Kay, she looked straight at her and her voice . . . ' Mrs Bramley paused before adding: ' "My baby's lost!" she said; and those were the last words she ever spoke. Shortly after she was removed to a hospital and my aunt never saw her again except . . . ' She broke off as if to draw breath and then said in a more level tone: 'The war ended and my aunt married an American and went to live in the States. It was ten years before she returned to England and told my mother about that wartime experience.'

Mrs Bramley's voice had dropped to a low tone, which I found vaguely oppressive as she said:

'That isn't the end of the story. Despite her new life in America, and the love she had for her husband, my aunt was never able to be happy for long. She was haunted, you see, by the sight from time to time of that poor bereaved mother sitting staring out of a window, and she believed she could hear her sad voice saying: "My baby's lost!" My aunt believed she was asking her to help find the baby for her.'

Despite my feeling of apprehension, I could not stop myself asking if her aunt was still 'haunted'. Mrs Bramley looked at me with a strangely furtive expression in her eyes. It was a minute or two before she said:

'No, she isn't. You see she had told my mother, Katherine, the story and from then on, it was as if the haunting had passed to her. A year ago my mother died but before she passed away, she told me and . . . and since then I have never been free. Maybe now . . .' her voice trailed into silence and she turned away from me and stared out of the window.

Suddenly, without warning, I felt an intense, inexplicable dislike for my travelling companion. The feeling was totally irrational for had I not, after all, done my utmost to persuade her to tell me that story? I picked up my newspaper and pretended to be engrossed in it although I'd read it all long since. The more I thought about the 'hauntings', the more bizarre they seemed. Old people did tend to exaggerate their wartime experiences. Emotions at that time must have been greatly heightened and with so many deaths, perhaps people needed to believe their loved ones were not really so far away but ghosts in another room. It was a sad little story, I told myself firmly, but so improbable, I should not allow it to bother me.

Several years have passed since that long train journey and I only recall Mrs Bramley's face with difficulty—and with that same irrational dislike. You see, although Martin and I are still deeply in love and we have a baby on the way, in the quiet hours of the night when I'm least expecting it, the ghost she talked about comes to haunt me now. Sometimes I see the shadow of a hunched, weeping figure sitting by my window and I hear a sad little voice saying to me: 'My baby's lost!' I believe that old woman knew when she spoke of a chain, that somehow she would be making me part of it, and by unburdening herself, she would pass on her haunting.

Now you have read this story, I can't help hoping your name is Katherine, Kitty, Kay or Kathy because then you, too, might become one of the links, and I shall be left in peace.

14.

Turning Point
Deception

Phillipa glanced sideways at her 'In' tray. Moira, her secretary, had just dumped another pile of manuscripts on top of the existing ones, thus sending Phillipa's hopes of a short afternoon into oblivion.

Why, she asked herself, did her workload always seem to get larger in the children's holidays? Why, for heaven's sake, couldn't the pressure come when they were safely tucked away in school and she could cope comparatively easily with her job? Was her mother right in saying that she was crazy to go back to work whilst Lizzie and Josh were so young?

Resentment of this guilt-inspiring parental interference burned in Phillipa's throat and for a moment she allowed herself to relive all those salient arguments—they needed the money she put into the kitty. Now, even with the expense of an *au pair*, they could save enough for a decent holiday. Everyone else's kids had been to Centre Park, Disneyland, Spain . . . and Jerry had agreed. He didn't mind having an *au pair* in the spare room. The kids didn't mind having to camp in sleeping bags in their parents' room when anyone came to stay. Besides, she was bored to tears with housework, nappies, Blue Peter and Playdough and she'd loved her job . . . was good at it.

'But children need their mother . . .'

So, maybe she did feel guilty from time to time; maybe she did panic from time to time; maybe she did have doubts about the capability of an eighteen-year-old Italian student to cope with the children, especially Lizzie who at seven was . . . well, demanding . . . and yes, probably the kids did see far too much telly, but . . .

With a sigh, Phillipa picked up her pen and drew the first of the manuscripts out of the tray, and putting all thoughts of her children firmly out of her mind, applied herself to her work.

*   *   *

'Well, did she say why she can't take us to the park? She said she would and it isn't raining!'

Josh screwed up his nose and shrugged his shoulders.

'She said she was washing her hair.'

Lizzie's scowl deepened.

'She did that yesterday. *I'm bored!*'

'She said we could watch telly,' Josh proffered without enthusiasm.

'That's what she always says when she

117

doesn't want to play with us. I bet she's going out with her boyfriend tonight! I bet they do it.'

'Do what?' Josh asked, kicking at a dormant Power Ranger with his toe.

'You're too young!' His sister said irritatingly.

'No, I'm not. Tell me.'

'You are, too, that's why you don't get sex lessons in the kindergarten, stupid. You have to be in my class. Anyway, you wouldn't understand.' As a matter of fact, Lizzie didn't understand either but she certainly did not intend to admit it.

'I hate Lucia. I hate her. I wish she was dead,' she muttered.

Josh's face brightened.

'We could shoot her with my space gun. Last week on Dr Who . . . '

'That's only pretend, silly,' his sister interrupted. 'Anyway, if you kill someone you'd be put in prison. The police would come and . . . '

' . . . and an ambulance. Di-dah! Di-dah! Di-dah!' Josh broke in excitedly.

'No, that's for injured people like on 999. That's what you have to dial when . . . ' Lizzie broke off, her brows furrowing together over the bridge of her nose as a brilliant idea to relieve the afternoon's boredom began to take root.

'If she was injured—like falling downstairs

118

or something—and only us here, we'd *have* to dial 999, and then a real ambulance would come and we could watch it from the window.'

Josh's face grew pink with excitement which quickly subsided. Experience had taught him that many of Lizzie's best ideas landed them both in trouble.

'But wouldn't They be cross when They found it wasn't true?' he asked uneasily.

'We'd say we dialled the numbers by mistake! Like when we tried to ring Mum last week.'

Josh was still not reassured.

'We're not s'posed to use the 'phone—only if we want Mummy in a real 'mergency. And then Lucia is s'posed to do it.'

Lizzie was not to be diverted.

'It *would* be a real emergency if we heard a big bang and *thought* she'd fallen downstairs.'

Satisfied, Josh made a dive for the telephone but Lizzie snatched it from him.

'It was my idea, I'm going to do it.'

Carefully, so that she wouldn't make a mistake, Lizzie dialled 999.

*   *   *

'Is that Mrs Phillipa Armstrong? This is WPC Williams here. Could you go home right away, Mrs Armstrong? We've just had a call from your daughter and it seems there has been an accident.'

119

Phillipa's face whitened and her hands clenched the receiver.

'Not Lizzie! Not Josh, my little boy . . . ?'

'No, not the children, Mrs Armstrong. It seems your *au pair* has fallen downstairs. The ambulance is on its way. Try not to worry. One of my colleagues has gone to your house to look after the children until you get home. Please try not to worry. It may not be as serious as your little girl seems to think. She was very calm although the little boy—Josh, isn't he?—he came on the 'phone and said there was a lot of blood. He said you'd be cross about the mess it was making on the carpet.'

'But what about my *au pair*, Lucia?' Phillipa asked frantically. 'Didn't you speak to her?'

'No, Madam, your daughter said she had locked herself in her bedroom so she could have mysterics. We took this to mean "hysterics"', she added, without a hint of humour. 'I think you should leave right away. Do you have transport? We can send a police car . . . '

'No, no, I have my car. I'll be about half an hour . . . '

As she raced to the lift, Phillipa prayed that she would not have to stop to be sick.

* * *

Jerry looked at his wife's exhausted face and bent to kiss the top of her head.

'Honestly, darling, you really mustn't let this get you down. After all, nothing terrible happened, did it?'

Phillipa sniffed and dabbed at her eyes.

'*You* weren't here! *You* didn't have to try and explain things to the policeman and the ambulance men and hear all that stuff about fines and imprisonment for making false calls and . . . Jerry, if you go on grinning like that I'll . . . I'll . . . '

'You could push me downstairs and then Lizzie could justifiably dial 999 . . . '

'Jerry! It's no laughing matter.'

He patted her hand.

'I know, I know, but even you laughed when you told me how serious the policeman sounded when you told him about Lucia's "mysterics".'

'I'm not laughing now,' Phillipa said. 'Lizzie . . . '

'Lizzie was suitably impressed by that telling-off she got and when I tucked her up,' Jerry interrupted gently, 'I told her there'd be no telly for two weeks. Needless to say, she wasn't so upset about that as the fact that Josh wasn't getting the same punishment, but she knows as well as I do that Josh doesn't have the same imagination she has. After all, Pips, your daughter takes after you so you can't really blame her. And they *were* "odiously" bored.'

'Odiously' Phillipa repeated. 'Another one

121

she got out of the dictionary, I suppose.'

Jerry nodded. 'Told me it meant "terribly". She needs more mental in-put than she's getting.'

Phillipa grimaced.

'I suppose you're right. You can guess what Mum said: "If you'd been there, Pippa, instead of . . . "'

'Now don't start feeling guilty, Pips. You've as much right to a career as I have. Maybe I should be the one to stay at home.'

'That's crazy. You earn ten times more than I do. Besides, I'm willing to admit Mum's right about one thing—we don't really need the extra money. I mean, the kids love the caravan in Devon and, I didn't tell Mum this, but the job isn't as much fun as I'd thought it would be. And half the time, I'm worrying about the children. Suppose one of them really had fallen downstairs. Lucia wouldn't have coped—not the way Lizzie did. That WPC said she was wonderful the way she gave our address and looked up my telephone number and . . . I suppose I'll have to start looking for another *au pair* now that Lucia's gone. God knows what awful stories that girl's going to tell her cousin when she gets to London. Honestly, darling, I'm beginning to think Mum's right after all. Maybe in a year or two when Lizzie and Josh are both in school until much later in the day, I could think again about my career. But will I regret it if I pack it in now?'

'That's for you to work out. Isn't there a compromise? Couldn't you work part time? Or better still, get a computer and work here? Maybe they'll let you do copy-editing or proof reading at home? Why don't you sleep on it? In the morning, it'll all seem much clearer. By the way, I love you!'

'I love you, too!' Phillipa said as she followed him upstairs. Glancing in at the children, their faces blissfully innocent in sleep, she knew she did not have to wait until morning. The turning point had come.

15.

The Affair
Acumen

Across the breakfast table, her husband said:

'I may be late home tonight. I have a meeting at five. It'll probably drag on with that fool, Geoffrey Benson, talking round in circles. There's nothing on, is there?'

She shook her head. No, there was nothing on—nothing to relieve the boredom of another long evening watching television; no good film at the local cinema; no dinner party; nothing but the same old rubbish on the BBC.

She put the cereal packets into the sideboard, poured herself another cup of coffee and lit a cigarette. She waited for Oliver's customary remark. It came.

'You ought to eat something, Jane. And to cut out that smoking!'

But the expected comment had lost its power to irritate her. There was even some satisfaction in waiting for the inevitable and having it presented on time.

She said nothing. There was nothing more she could say to Oliver—nothing that could be voiced aloud. For some time now, all the things she wanted to say to him went on inside her head. Right now a voice was saying: That's the last time I'll hear you say that to me,

Oliver. Soon I won't need to smoke. Soon I'll be free of the dull domesticity of married life; for ten years I've cleaned and shopped and ironed for you and I'm sick to death of it all. I thought when I married you it would be different.

It was hard to pinpoint the exact moment when the exciting days of newly married life had begun to fade into dull routine; hard to say exactly when Oliver had started to behave like a husband and ceased to be the ardent attentive lover. Maybe if she'd known when that crack in harmony had started, she could have prevented their marriage from crumbling altogether. When she had married Oliver at seventeen, she had believed she could truly live with him 'happily ever after'. Not for them the quarrels and disillusionments and divorces in which other people became involved. She and Oliver were going to have a perfect marriage, just the two of them happy ever after . . .

Now it was all over.

'I'll try not to be too late!' Oliver's voice broke in on her thoughts.

It didn't matter how late home he was this evening, she thought, because she would be with Sebastian. Sebastian loved her the way Oliver once loved her. When her husband came back home from his dull old meeting, she would be gone . . .

'Well, what do you think, Jane?'

She looked up quickly, meeting his puzzled stare.

'I'm sorry, I didn't hear what you said!'

He's changed! she thought inconsequently. He's only just forty and yet he seems years older. He wants me to be old, too. He likes our marriage to be solid and dependable and dull.

'I said I thought you ought to see Doctor Jarvis. You don't look at all well.'

She gave a sigh of irritation.

'I'm perfectly all right, Oliver. Don't fuss!'

I don't need a doctor to cure me, the voice in her head told her. I need Sebastian. I need what Sebastian will give me—lots and lots of love and fun and laughter. Sebastian makes me feel seventeen again.

'Now look here, Jane, I'm going to insist you see Jarvis . . .'

'*I'm all right, Oliver!*' she heard herself shouting and quickly brought her voice down several tones. 'Really, I'm quite all right.'

'I'll try not to be too late,' he said.

A few minutes later he had collected his briefcase and was gone with a parting mumbled threat to discuss her health further when he got home.

But she wouldn't be there!

She went upstairs to her bedroom . . . only it wasn't *her* bedroom. It was Oliver's, too. Their night clothes lay strewn over the twin beds. Oliver's pyjama cord had come out and he had asked her to thread it back. She thought: I'll

126

do it before I go. It'll be the last thing I'll ever do for him.

She sat on her bed and performed the task with more than her usual care. When it was done, she bathed and dressed and began to make the bed, wash up breakfast and tidy the flat. At eleven o'clock, her daily help arrived to do the cleaning. Today Jane said to her:

'If I wanted you for longer, Mrs May, could you manage it?'

'I dare say I could fit it in afternoons, Mrs Fisher. How long would you be wanting me extra like?'

'I . . . I'm not sure. I'll let you know.'

Jane drank her coffee and looked at the woman gratefully. Afternoons would 'suit' very well. In the afternoons Mrs May could come in, clean up, and prepare Oliver's supper. Women liked looking after bachelors. Oliver was not fussy about his food and Mrs May would feel sorry for him. She might even do his mending.

She felt easier now that she knew someone would be replacing her.

There's nothing to keep me here now, she thought with rising excitement.

After Mrs May had gone, she read the paper and prepared herself a salad which she couldn't eat. She wasn't due at Sebastian's flat until four, so she deliberately delayed packing her suitcase until half past two. It would give her something to do in the last minutes. Never before having walked out on her husband to go to live with a lover, she wasn't sure how it would be at the moment of leaving.

In the end, she was nearly late. It was ten minutes past four when she took a last look at herself in the mirror.

I don't look like me, she thought. I look like someone else—someone young and beautiful on the threshold of a new life.

The letter to Oliver was propped against the mirror. She straightened it and turned her back on the room.

'Goodbye!' she said aloud. But somehow the moment held none of the expected drama, pathos—not even a shadow of passing regret at the finish of her life with Oliver.

In the taxi, she puzzled over her reactions.

Can ten years of marriage be wiped out so simply? she thought. Oliver did love me and I loved him. Where has it all gone, the fun, the passion, the excitement? Why aren't I feeling sad, regretful, guilty at ending it all like this?

But all she felt was a slight shock because it had been so easy to close the door on the past.

*   *   *

Across the breakfast table, Oliver stared at his wife's head bent over the bowl of cereal she was only pretending to eat. He couldn't see her face. He said:

'I may be late home tonight. I've a meeting

128

at five. It'll probably drag on with that fool, Benson, talking round in circles. There's nothing on, is there?'

She shook her head. He thought: She might at least answer me. She won't even look at me this morning. Is this to be THE DAY? *Jane, don't do it. It isn't just that I love you and I need you. He's no good. Sebastian has one woman after another and they don't mean anything to him. Don't let him fool you into believing he loves you. He doesn't know what love is. You'll be just another conquest. Jane . . .*

She was lighting another cigarette—the third since they had got up. He said:

'You ought to eat something, Jane. And cut out that smoking!'

But what was the use of saying so day after day? She smoked because her nerves were in shreds; because she couldn't make up her mind whether to leave him or not.

Maybe it would be better to have it out? To tell her that he knew she'd been lunching with Sebastian nearly every day for the last month? Why couldn't she see for herself that these were Sebastian's usual tactics—the softening up process and then, when he was sure of success, the grab to be followed by a few weeks of bliss and then the kill . . .

Oliver felt sick. That mustn't happen to Jane—not to his Jane. If only he could be sure whether she had the strength to resist what so many other women had succumbed to. She didn't look very strong—at least, not physically. She looked ill. He said:

'I really think it would be a good idea if you let Jarvis give you a thorough over-haul. I think you need a holiday. We both do, really. Perhaps we could go abroad for a couple of weeks next month—Italy, maybe. We always promised ourselves a second honeymoon and we never had it. What do you think, Jane?'

She hadn't heard a word. He said again:

'I think you ought to see Doctor Jarvis. You don't look at all well.'

She was lighting another cigarette.

'I'm all right, Oliver. Don't fuss!'He knew she was anxious for him to leave. He made one last effort.

'Now look here, Jane, I'm going to insist you see Jarvis . . . '

Her tone as she argued that she was perfectly all right shocked him. Now he was really afraid. If she could use that near hysterical cry of exasperation, she must have stopped loving him. He nearly broke his resolve then . . . nearly went to her to beg her to listen to him. *Don't go! Don't go! Don't go!'* The words hammered in his head but he overcame the momentary weakness. He had to trust her. If he couldn't do that, it would never be the same between them again.

'I'll try not to be too late,' he said.

Slowly he reached for his briefcase and let himself out of the flat.

＊　　　＊　　　＊

After all, she was early—too early. Sebastian had not arrived. Jane looked round the flat with growing nervousness. She'd never been there before although Sebastian had often invited her. Everything was so different from her own home. Sebastian was very modern—the decor was stark and brilliant. There was a chromium cocktail bar in one corner of the room, the latest wide-screen television in another, and a music system with a stack of CDs and tapes beneath the window.

She thought stupidly: I like classical music—the ballet, proms. I'm a hopeless dancer. I don't even like drinking much. Suppose Sebastian gets bored with me?

She glanced at her watch. Four-twenty. He'd said he wouldn't be here until half past four; maybe even five.

'Here's the key, my darling. Let yourself in and make yourself comfortable. You'll find everything you want.'

She crossed the room and went into the adjoining bedroom.

There were flowers on the bedside table—a note beside them saying as romantically as she could have wished, the one simple word *'Tonight!'.* Her cheeks burned. She stood looking down at the scarlet blooms and thought stupidly: Oliver would laugh!

In the bathroom were face tissues, bath oil, and emerald green, voluminous, voluptuous bath towels to match the green and gold decor.

Nervously, she lit a cigarette and went back into the bedroom. She looked at the clock on the bedside table and realised only a few minutes had passed. She thought: Hurry up, Sebastian. I'm afraid . . .

Hanging on the back of the door was a navy blue, white piped silk dressing gown. As she stared at it, it began to take on Sebastian's shape. She could see his slim young body and above it, the unlined handsome face and long thick dark hair. He was so young, half Oliver's age. She had never allowed herself to worry about it before, but now she faced the fact that she was all of ten years older than Sebastian.

She stood up and walked across to the mirror. This looking-glass was different. The one at home reflected the Jane she wanted to be—pretty, desirable, *young*. Sebastian's mirror showed her as she really was—her face still unlined but nevertheless that of a woman nearing thirty; a woman with ten years of marriage behind her; ten years of growing up.

She thought: If I'd had a child when Oliver wanted, it would be five years old. I'd be a mother.

But she hadn't had Oliver's child and now suddenly, here in Sebastian's flat, she knew why. She didn't want to give up her girlhood; to grow up; to grow old. And that was why she was here now, waiting for a young boy who had the power to make her feel seventeen again; to give her back her youth.

'I don't really love him at all!'

She sat down at the dressing table and heard the ticking of the bedside clock. Time was passing; Sebastian would be here soon; time never stood still and it wasn't going to stop while she made up her mind about her future. Was it possible to turn back the clock? Could she find again with Sebastian that which she had failed to keep alive with Oliver?

Suddenly she realised the truth. Oliver had grown from a carefree, fun-loving boy to become a responsible, caring, devoted husband. It was she who had failed—failed to keep up with him—to put her self-centred girlhood behind her.

Perhaps it wasn't too late even now. If she hurried . . . if his dull old meeting went on long enough, she could be home before him, burn the note and he'd never know. *He need never know.* Perhaps she could persuade him to take her abroad for a holiday, far, far away from Sebastian. They might even have that second honeymoon. If she hurried . . .

*   *   *

He saw the envelope by the mirror and for a long time he stood there, his heart beating painfully as he stared at it. Then, without

133

touching it, he went down to the kitchen and poured himself a drink.

So he had lost after all! He'd felt it in his bones all day—that niggling, nagging sensation that he must get home early or something terrible would happen. He'd cut the meeting with Benson, no longer caring what his boss would say to him the next morning. He'd rather a thousand times over lose his job than lose Jane.

He tried to pinpoint the moment where it had all gone wrong. They'd been so happy at first—young, carefree, and desperately in love. They'd pitied the couples all around them who nagged one another and quarrelled and parted or were unfaithful. It could never happen to them.

But it had happened. No nagging, no quarrels, but she had left him all the same. Perhaps the thought would have been more bearable if she had gone to a better man, but Sebastian was a mere boy; shallow, irresponsible, incapable of loving Jane the way she needed love. She was so young still. She needed to be protected from life. He'd known for ages that she wasn't ready yet to accept the realities in place of the dreams. Perhaps he had been wrong not to insist on their having a family. But Jane hadn't wanted a baby and he had believed there was still plenty of time.

Now there was no more time. The hands of the clock had spun round faster than he had reckoned. Jane had gone.

He heard the key in the front door and jumped to his feet. The desire to know instantly if it was Jane, was tempered by the knowledge that he mustn't go into the hall; mustn't know about Sebastian.

'You're home early after all, Oliver!' Her voice came clearly from the hall. So she had seen his briefcase.

'Just having a drink!' he called back.

'Be down in a minute—going to tidy up!'

Her high heels clattered on the tiles before being muffled by the stair carpet. The bedroom door clicked shut. There was silence. Presently, she came down. She looked very pale and her hands were trembling.

He gave her a glass of wine.

'This thundery weather is exhausting!' he said. 'I cut the meeting short and came home. First thing I did was plonk myself down in a chair and pour myself a stiff drink.'

She was staring at the rim of her glass.

'So you didn't go upstairs . . . for a wash, to change? Usually you . . . '

'I know. I was too whacked. I'll go up now.'

He went up the stairs a second time, his heart a painful mixture of apprehension and hope when he opened the bedroom door.

Now his heart was singing as he stared across the room. The envelope on the mantelpiece had gone.

16.

The Anniversary
Love

It had been a humdinger of a row . . . the worst
they had yet had, and like most of the others,
over something so unimportant that once he
had cooled down, he wondered how it could
ever have reached such absurd proportions.

'You simply don't care about me any more.
If you really loved me . . . '

Nerily's voice had sounded close to tears
and he might have lost some of his anger if she
had not ended with yet another unfair
accusation: '. . . you'd make the effort to come
and see me the way you used to before we
were married . . . '

She knew perfectly well that it was not a
matter of choice whether he went home or not.
He had spelt it out to her before he had
agreed to go on the eight-week, live-in course
that would mean promotion for him if he did
well. At the time, she had agreed that of
course he must grab the opportunity; that she
could manage perfectly well on her own, and
she had happily enthused about the fact that
his boss must think highly of him to have
selected him for this chance.

'I'm terribly proud of you, Chris!'

A little of his former resentment returned at the memory. He was, he told himself as he pocketed his mobile phone and continued his short walk to the village pub, more than justified in accusing her of selfishness and unfairness, and in warning her that she was rapidly becoming a whinger of the first order. She knew perfectly well that he was working his guts out not for himself but to give her and the twins Tom and James a decent life. It had been tough going since Nerily had had to give up her job to look after the twins. After all, she had been the one who had most wanted a baby! Not that he didn't love the boys every bit as much as she did—perhaps even more. There were times when she got fed up spooning food into their mouths, changing dirty nappies and having broken nights whilst the poor little devils cut their teeth. They had shared the chores when he'd been at home, but for the past month he'd not been around at weekends and evenings to help. It wasn't just that home was a hell of a long way away— a good three-hour drive and only a Sunday in which to get there and back—there was the expense. Nerily knew exactly how costly petrol was and although his boss had allowed him the use of a company car whilst he was here on the outskirts of Manchester, he still had to pay for the fuel.

As the pub came into sight, he slowed his pace, unwilling yet to join the other chaps on the course for a pint or two after work as had become their custom these past four weeks. The trouble was, he felt utterly miserable when he and Nerily rowed. Although she didn't believe it, he loved her every bit as much as on the day he had married her and he hated the thought that he'd made her cry. Surely she realized that he wanted to see her every bit as much as she wanted to see him? It was all so silly!

'Our fifth wedding anniversary, and you promised that we'd never, ever miss the day even if you had to cross the whole world to get to me!'

Well, he had made that wild promise when they were on their honeymoon. It was the sort of thing one said without really thinking about it. Suppose he'd been on active service in Iraq! Of course there were bound to be unavoidable times when they couldn't celebrate on exactly the right date. Why couldn't Nerily be reasonable and realize that this was one of them?

*   *   *

'I'll never forgive him for turning off his phone,' Nerily told herself as she shoved another load of the boys' clothes into the washing machine. 'Chris would never have done a thing like that in the old days. It just goes to show how right I was—he doesn't care any more; at least, not in the way I care. If he really loved me . . . '

She brushed the tears angrily from her eyes and carried the twins up to bed. For once they were both ready to settle down to sleep almost at once and she was able to return to the kitchen to pour herself a drink and, hopefully, calm down. As the anger evaporated, misery took its place. She hated it when she and Chris rowed. It was always over something really stupid like where she had put his blue socks or why she had left his best screwdriver out in the rain! Mostly, they agreed on all the important things.

Tears threatened once more as she recalled his accusations that she was selfish, unfair, whingeing. What was so selfish about wanting him to come home for their anniversary, for heaven's sake?

Was she being unreasonable to expect him to make the trip? He didn't finish work on a Friday until six o'clock and had to be back by nine on Saturday morning. With a three-hour drive, it would be nine before he arrived home and he would have to leave again at six in the morning—and with a clear head. Whereas if she were to drive up to Manchester . . .

Suddenly Nerily knew exactly what she was going to do. She would ask her sister, Sue, if she would have the twins for the night. Then she could leave home early and drive up to Manchester on Friday arriving at six. She and

Chris could be together until just before nine next morning. Why on earth hadn't either of them thought of this solution before? All she needed to do was to find somewhere for them to stay for the night, book a room and then present Chris with a *fait accompli*. She could imagine his look of pleasure when she turned up without warning—his face crinkling up the way it always did when he was happy. It made her happy just to think about it. I'll ring Sue now, she thought, and reached for the 'phone.

*   *   *

It was not until Friday morning as he dressed and shaved that Chris decided he had been all kinds of a fool. It only needed a little effort and he could give Nerily the most wonderful surprise. He'd ask his instructor if he could miss the last class so that he could leave at five instead of six. He'd be home by eight and that would give Nerily time to get into her glad-rags and for them to be on their way to their favourite restaurant by nine. Plenty of time to eat and tell her how much he still loved her—and always would! And later, they'd make love.

The anticipation of her pleasure in his surprise was enough to restore his own happiness. He'd not really had a moment's peace of mind since their row on the 'phone two days ago. Now, in twelve hours' time, he'd open the front door and when she ran into his arms, he'd kiss her as she had never been kissed before. It made him happy just to think about it.

* * *

At five o'clock, the phone rang in Sue's house. It was Chris on his mobile.

'I'm on my way home, Sue—a surprise for Nerily. It's our anniversary, as you probably know. Anyway, I just thought I ought to check that she isn't going out to the cinema or anything. You haven't been asked to baby-mind the twins, have you?'

Sue's face paled. 'On your way, you said? Oh, Chris!'

'What's that supposed to mean? Is Nerily out? Where are the boys?'

'Here with me!' Sue replied, trying frantically to think. All that filled her mind was the thought of the two of them passing en route on the M5, each hoping to surprise the other. 'I'm looking after them. Nerily isn't here,' she gabbled on. 'Look, Chris, something rather awful has happened . . . I mean, it's awkward. I don't know what to say. I promised Nerily that if you rang, I wouldn't tell you where she was. I gave her my solemn promise. Look, Chris, there isn't much point you coming back if Nerily isn't here, is there? She said she would ring me around six-ish to see if the boys were okay. I'll ask her then if I can tell you where she is.'

Chris' voice was taut.

'I don't want to know . . . and frankly, I don't care, come to that. She might at least have stayed home knowing I'd be bound to telephone her. After all, it IS our wedding anniversary. When she phones, you can tell her I'm going down to the pub.'

'Don't do that, Chris, please. Just wait till I can ring you back, please?'

'I'd planned this as a surprise and it's pretty disappointing to say the least to have it thrown back in my face. Sorry to involve you, but don't bother any more. Just tell Nerily I would have made the effort, as she put it, but now I'm glad I didn't. I'm off to the pub to get very, very drunk and if I remember, I'll drink a toast to her. 'Bye now! Be good!'

* * *

It was nearly seven o'clock when Sue received the expected telephone call from Nerily. Far from sounding despairing, her voice was ecstatic.

'The trip only took me two and three quarter hours . . . there wasn't a single hold-up so I got here just as Chris was going to the pub. Oh, Sue, we can't stop thinking how awful it would have been if we'd missed each other. Can you imagine us passing each other on the motorway? It would have been the most terrible disaster.'

Sue smiled.

'It's only an anniversary, not your wedding you'd have missed, honey!'

But for Nerily and Chris it was like their wedding day all over again.

17.

The Boyfriend
Duplicity

She woke up with a severe headache and an absolute certainty that everything would go wrong. She reached out for the cup of tea Paul was handing to her and with the other hand reached for the Paracetamol bottle. Her husband sat down on the edge of the bed and watched her grimace as she swallowed two of the pills.

'Bad night?'

She nodded, letting her head fall back for a few more seconds of precious relaxation before 'The Day' began.

'I dreamed every conceivable nightmare known to women,' she said, attempting to smile. 'The cake dropped in the middle, the bread turned out to be mouldy, the flowers all wilted in their vases and Sam turned up to supper in his pyjamas. It was awful!'

Paul laughed.

'Dreams always go by opposites. Anyway, Sam in his pyjamas is very often more presentable than Sam in his jeans.'

'You forget he's only ten!' Annabel defended her youngest. Her words were automatic. Neither she nor Paul were worried about Sam.

'Look, darling, don't you think you may be making too big a Thing of this visit?' Paul's eyes were serious, thoughtful. 'I mean, you're practically on the edge of a nervous breakdown and Linda's like an over wound mainspring. After all, we don't even KNOW this fellow is so special, do we?'

Annabel looked at her husband with a mixture of love and feminine exasperation at his male obtuseness.

'Of course I know,' she said, sitting up purposefully.

Paul gave her a puzzled sideways glance.

'But you said Linda was off-hand—casual about the boy.'

Annabel sighed.

'Yes, I know. But there've been a hundred and one signs since she asked if he could come and stay a night. Any woman who has ever been in love would recognise them.'

Her husband raised his eyebrows.

'Oh? What signs?'

'Well, dropping odd remarks about what we're having to eat and would it help if she turned out the spare room to save me the bother; and couldn't Sam be told once in a while that it's rude to make personal remarks and why can't he be made to clean his fingernails.'

'Why not, indeed!' Paul said laughing. 'What you're trying to say is that Linda is keen we all make a good impression. But I don't see how that proves she's serious about the boy. She never told you she was, did she, though it's weeks now since she met him.'

'But that's exactly it!' Annabel said, pushing back the bedclothes and swinging her feet to the floor. 'She has raved about all the others until we all thought we'd go crazy hearing their names. This one—well, it's just because she can't bring herself to tell me how important it is that I know it IS important.'

'Feminine logic!' Paul said and disappeared into the bathroom.

Sam came into the bedroom, face shining, hair tousled and waved a hand beneath Annabel's face.

'Look!' he said. 'A quid! Linda gave it to me.'

Annabel gave her youngest a quick glance.

'It's for promising not to talk to the fellow what's coming to stay.' He bounced happily on the mattress.

'*Who* is coming to stay, not *what*!' Annabel corrected him automatically. 'And what do you mean, not talk to him?'

'It's a bribe—to be seen and not heard,' Sam said cheerfully. 'I say, Mum, is she going to marry this guy?'

'Of course not!' she replied with a conviction she was far from holding.

I'm being silly! she told herself, shooing Sam back to his room to get dressed. If I'm not careful I'll end up botching today just by being

146

over-nervous myself.

They had the usual family breakfast, later than normal because it was Saturday and neither Paul nor Linda went to work. Linda ate nothing and Annabel omitted her usual plea for her to have at least one piece of toast. Sam miraculously refrained from mentioning Linda's bribe and Linda refrained from mentioning the boyfriend, Royston. Only Paul seemed completely himself. Before going out to the garden he asked Linda what time her boyfriend was arriving.

'Twelve fifteen train!' she told him and blushed in a way Annabel had not seen since Linda's schooldays. She fled from the room and Annabel was left alone with a grinning Sam. There were cornflakes on his chin.

'When will you grow up?' she asked, throwing him a napkin. But she knew suddenly that she didn't in the least want him to grow up. Why couldn't Linda say exactly what was on her mind the way Sam did! Why couldn't Linda say: *'I've asked Royston down to meet you all. He's special, important'*? Why couldn't she be a little girl again with cornflakes on her chin? Now they were shut off from each other—unable to communicate except on superficial levels.

Why don't I just ask her outright, Annabel thought, depressed as she made Sam's bed and removed a sticky sweet paper from his lampshade? Why can't I just say: *'Are you in*

147

*love with him, darling?'*Because she'll tell me when she's ready to tell me, she thought, answering her own question. If she hasn't told me, it's because she doesn't want me to know. It's her life.

When Royston finally arrived, an arm tucked possessively through Linda's, she was unprepared for his tall, dark handsomeness; for the manly look; for his self assurance as Linda introduced her to him and he smiled and said 'Hi!' as if he'd met her a dozen times before.

She escaped to the kitchen, telling Linda to call her father in from the garden—the men might like a beer before lunch.

Removing the foil to allow the chicken to crisp up, Annabel attempted to marshal her thoughts into some kind of coherence. Royston couldn't be more than twenty-two or three. He was still a university student, only a few years older than Linda.

But old enough to want to get married, she thought. They were both old enough. Somewhere in the night, Linda had grown up—become a woman almost without her own mother noticing. The last boy Linda had brought home had seemed a boy—jeans, T-shirt, pop CDs and a broken skateboard. Royston was a fashionable young man-about-town, striped shirt, tight fitting jacket and smooth haircut. He exuded a pungent smell of after-shave.

I won't judge him on his clothes, she told herself sharply. She wondered if Paul would feel self-conscious about his old-fashioned grey trousers and golf shirt.

Sam burst into the kitchen.

'I say, Mum, Dad's just offered Linda's fellow a beer but he wants whisky and there isn't any. He says he doesn't drink beer. He'd like a glass of milk instead.'

Affectation! Annabel thought and then decided she was being unreasonable. Maybe the boy had a duodenal. She poured out a glass of milk.

Confounding her nightmare premonitions, the lunch was cooked to perfection. Paul kept up a flow of conversation despite their guest's ill-concealed boredom with Paul's choice of subjects.

'Sorry, I don't play golf.' 'No, I can't bring myself to appreciate cats.' 'I don't care for gardening. I prefer town life.'

It seemed as if Royston had little in common with their family. What then had he in common with Linda who was a passionate country and animal lover?

On Saturday afternoons Paul became a TV sports addict. Royston seemed very bored so Linda took him for a walk. Sam helped Annabel wash the dishes . . . at least, he dried them.

'Royston didn't offer to help clear the table nor anything!' he remarked laconically. 'I say,

149

Mum, I thought of a joke at lunch. It's "Royston doesn't dig gardens." Get it?'

'No, I don't!' said Annabel. Sam's jokes were often difficult to understand. Their explanation was often even more difficult to follow.

'You know, Mum—dig. It means to go for. Royston doesn't go for gardens, doesn't dig them, see?'

'Yes!' said Annabel. It wasn't funny but she laughed. She laughed a little too long and nearly cried.

Linda and Royston were late back to tea. Linda looked flushed.

'Try some of Linda's chocolate cake,' Paul said, handing a fair sized slice to Royston. 'She makes a very good sponge!'

'Do you cook as well, Beautiful?' Royston asked, touching Linda's arm. Linda drew her arm away quickly, blushing. She didn't look happy. Sam was stifling a giggle. Linda shot him a fierce warning glance.

'What's the laugh, Freckles?' Royston asked. His voice lacked warmth. Sam's mouth tightened. He was sensitive about his freckles and came in for more than his fair share of teasing at school.

Linda made a halting attempt to explain. Royston's dark perfectly shaped brows rose above the deep-set dark eyes.

'Do the kid good to be teased occasionally,' he said.

'But not too often!' Paul said quietly. Annabel knew then that Paul didn't like him.

Nor do I, she thought, oh, nor do I!

Only Sam spoke his thoughts—after Royston had taken Linda out to dinner.

'I just hope she doesn't marry *him*!' he said as he settled down to watch telly.

Later, as they were preparing for bed, Annabel said to Paul:

'Perhaps we'd be prejudiced against any boy Linda wanted to marry. Parents never think anyone good enough for their offspring.'

'She won't marry him!' Paul said soothingly and then spoilt it all by adding: 'At least, I very much hope not.'

They didn't come home until after two. Annabel, sleepless, heard their whispering voices in the hall. Presently, Royston's steps passed her door on the way to the spare room. Linda tiptoed to her own room and thoughtfully switched out the hall light. So few years ago, she would have put her head round Annabel's door and whispered: 'I'm back, Mum. I had a fabulous time!'

Had she had a fabulous time tonight? Was she even now starry-eyed, dreaming in front of her mirror, thinking about a future with Royston when they didn't have to end the night in separate rooms?

'What's wrong, Pudge?' In the darkness Paul's arm encircled her.

'I want her to have someone kind and gentle

151

and good, like you!' she whispered. 'I want her to be happy, Paul, the same way you and I have been happy. I want . . . '

'I know, darling. Stop worrying. And don't cry. It hasn't happened yet!'

Sunday was Friday's nightmare come true. Unknown to her, the calor gas cylinder ran out and by the time Paul had switched to the spare, the Sunday joint was ruined.

'Oh, dear!' Annabel cried as Paul carved the first uneatable slices. 'I am sorry. I'll make something else—omelettes. Will that do?'

'Fine!' said Paul.

'Super!' said Sam.

'Yes, of course,' said Linda. 'I'll help.'

'Don't bother on my account,' said Royston. 'I'm really not hungry.'

She felt guilty cooking the omelettes; embarrassed eating them when Royston's plate remained empty.

'Have some cheese!' Paul suggested.

'Thanks, but I'm really not hungry,' Royston repeated.

'Have a glass of milk,' Sam said. It wasn't meant to be one of his jokes but Linda laughed. It was a high, brittle laugh.

'Yes, have a glass of milk!' she said. 'Good for the complexion.'

He left after tea. Paul drove him to the station. Linda had managed to sprain her ankle going upstairs or coming down them and said she couldn't go with them.

'Poor sweet!' Royston said as he kissed her goodbye in the hall. 'As soon as it's better you must come up to town for a really good weekend. Be fun, don't you think?'

'Yes!' she said. 'See you!'

'So long!' he waved to Annabel. He never thanked her for the perfectly cooked chicken, nor the ruined joint.

As the car disappeared down the drive Sam emerged from the sanctuary of his bedroom.

'Cripes!' he said. 'Thank the Lord he's gone. What a drip!'

'Sam!' his mother said reprovingly. She tried not to look at Linda's flushed face.

'Not a bad description of him really,' Linda said with studied casualness. 'Oh, well, now we can relax.'

Annabel followed her into the sitting room. She noticed maternally that Linda was not limping.

'Ankle okay again?' she asked.

Linda's taut face broke into a smile.

'Much!' she said. 'Funny how pains come and go. Like love. One minute you think you're crazy about someone and the next, you know you don't care if you never see them again. Hey, Freckles, you were very good. You earned your quid.'

'Okay, Beautiful!' Sam mimicked Royston's voice.

Annabel held her breath but there was no need, brother and sister were grinning at each

153

other.

'Well!' Annabel said, letting out her breath, 'I'd better get some supper. Dad will be hungry when he gets back.'

Paul came into the kitchen as she put the spaghetti Bolognese into a dish. He came over and kissed the warm nape of her neck.

'Looks good!' he said. 'Pity I don't eat spaghetti. I'll have a glass of milk instead.'

Annabel laughed.

'We mustn't be unkind, darling!' she said. 'Poor Royston! He's doomed to become the family joke now. We should be sorry for him.'

Paul was not smiling.

'Damned if I'll feel sorry for him' he said violently. 'After the rude, inconsiderate, boorish way he behaved to you, I could wring his smooth little neck. I . . . '

'Paul!' she hugged him into silence. 'Don't you see, we should be glad he behaved as he did? Linda was forced to see him the way he really is. Now it's all over, finished. She'll never marry *him*.'

Paul sighed.

'Well, I suppose you know what you're talking about. Did she *tell* you it was all off?'

'Well, no, not exactly, but I'm absolutely sure of it.'

'Feminine intuition?'

Annabel smiled.

'You can call it that!' she said.